BLOOD STAINS OF A SHOTTA 2

Lock Down Publications and Ca$h
Presents
BLOOD STAINS OF A SHOTTA 2
A Novel by *Jamaica*

Lock Down Publications
P.O. Box 870494
Mesquite, Tx 75187

First Edition March 2018
Printed in the United States of America

Lock Down Publications
Like our page on Facebook: Lock Down Publications @
www.facebook.com/lockdownpublications.ldp
Cover design and layout by: **Dynasty Cover Me**
Book interior design by: **Shawn Walker**
Edited by: **Sunny Giovanni**

Stay Connected with Us!

Text **LOCKDOWN** to 22828 to stay up-to-date with new releases, sneak peaks, contests and more…

Thank you!

Submission Guideline.

Submit the first three chapters of your completed manuscript to ldpsubmissions@gmail.com, subject line: Your book's title. The manuscript must be in a .doc file and sent as an attachment. Document should be in Times New Roman, double spaced and in size 12 font. Also, provide your synopsis and full contact information. If sending multiple submissions, they must each be in a separate email.

Have a story but no way to send it electronically? You can still submit to LDP/Ca$h Presents. Send in the first three chapters, written or typed, of your completed manuscript to:

LDP: Submissions Dept
Po Box 870494
Mesquite, Tx 75187

DO NOT send original manuscript. Must be a duplicate.

Provide your synopsis and a cover letter containing your full contact information.

Thanks for considering LDP and Ca$h Presents.

DEDICATION

Julia, Mama, I want to start out by letting you know that you're an amazing woman of God and person. If it wasn't for you, I don't know where I would be (tears). You inspire me to be better. I hope I can be half the woman that you are! You taught me everything, especially how to be a strong black woman. I can't stop crying writing this, grandma, mama, mother, I LOVE YOU!

CHAPTER 1
JAE

My life had been hell since that bloodclath shit happened to my man. I couldn't eat, sleep or breathe without Rocket at my side. For the first time in my life, I was scared. I paced the living room with Rocket's cellphone in my hand while my head was pounding due to a migraine from hell. It had been days, yet MooMoo hadn't stopped blowing up her father's phone, calling back to back.

"Hello?" I finally answered with tears gushing down my face.

"Jae, how are you?" she asked, yet she hadn't let me answer before she continued. "Where is my daddy?"

She was used to being with her dad on the weekends. It *was* the weekend. I held my breath hoping, my heart wouldn't give out on me. "Something—" I closed my eyes as I paused to get myself together. "Something bad happened to him." I couldn't get the rest of the words out.

"No! Not my daddy!" She screamed into the phone. "Why, Jae? Why?" She questioned me but I couldn't give her an answer.

I listened while we both cried our hearts out. Hot tears wet my lips.

After getting MooMoo off of the phone, I called Ashanti and let her know that I was on my way over there to see MiMi. It didn't take me no more than ten minutes to get to her spot.

"Jae!" MiMi answered the door with an innocent and beautiful smile on her face.

"How are you doing?" I scooped her up in my arms.

"Ready to go with you," she replied.

Ashanti stood back in the room, watching me closely while I interacted with her child, with a mean mug on her face that read, *I hate you, bitch.*

"You can't." I put her down on her feet.

"Why?" She looked up at me with water in her eyes, and it broke my heart.

I couldn't control my emotions or help the tears from falling from my eyes. I dropped to my knees and held her.

"What's wrong, Jae?" She pulled back from my chest and stared me dead in the face.

"Your daddy is..." I dropped my eyes from hers. "Hurt."

MiMi didn't ask anything else. She boo-hoo'd in my arms. Rocket was these girls' hero, their protector, their first love.

Ashanti stood back with a smile on her face when I delivered the news to MiMi. It took the grace of God to hold me back from not smoking that bitch right then and there in front of baby girl.

I embraced MiMi until she was calm. Devastation was visible all over her innocent face. "It's going to be okay." I wiped the tears away from her big brown eyes as I held her tighter in my arms.

"Promise?" she whispered in my ear.

Ashanti had yet to move or offer to comfort her child.

I pulled MiMi's face from my neck and held it lightly with both of my hands. "On everything I love, everything is going to be alright."

It was hard as fuck to leave the lil' lady, but I had to. It was time to go holla at Trap and find out if he had gotten any info on who tried to fold Rocket up.

A short while later, I linked up with him; he had been on a mission in the streets, trying to figure out who was courageous enough to pull the trigger on Rocket, but the streets wasn't responding.

"Niggas ain't sayin' shit, yo!" Trap's voice roared like thunder.

"Someone will, bruh. Someone will soon."

"Sis, I'ma find the nigga or whoever that did that shit!" Trap had tears in his eyes as he slammed my car door.

Rocket's father, OX, called me days after the shooting. He informed me that he had gotten my number from Ms. Judith and he had to hear the unspeakable details from me, himself.

"It's true, sis."

"Jae, no!" He yelled. "That's my only son, Jae," he said after I relayed to him what had taken place.

I knew the pain that he was going through. I'd witnessed it first-hand when my grandparents had to bury their first child. That shit killed them, mentally and emotionally, it drained them.

"It's gonna be okay," I told him. I needed to stay focused. I promised OX I would keep him up-to-date before I ended our conversation.

"Make sure you do," he pleaded.

"On my life," I vowed.

It didn't matter what I risked or lost, I was determined to do everything in a bitch's power to assure that OX didn't lose his son. And if he did, the city was going to be splattered with blood stains.

I would be a one bitch murdering crew. But little did I know there were others ready to ride just as hard as myself.

***

Gotti made a personal trip to see me. "You need twenty-four hours protection, Jae," he mentioned to me as he handed over the keys to the all-black 760 BMW.

"As long as mi ave dis," I pulled my 9-millimeter out of the waistline of my jeans, "mi gud." I had to let him know that as long as I had my 9, I was straight.

He smiled and told me he was just a call away if I needed him. "In the meantime, I'm going to take back control over The Heights."

I nodded. I had to let him do him.

"Call me if you need me," he preached as he let himself out.

As soon as the door closed, I rubbed my stomach as the tears cascaded down my face. I'd never encountered a situation where one minute I was made to feel like someone's life support, but in the blink of an eye, the plug is pulled and I was left feeling as if I flat-lined.

CHAPTER 2
RO

"What's the news saying?"

"The same thing it's been saying for the last three days, Ro. Nothing," my mother reported to me while sitting in front of the TV

We had called every-fucking hospital in Brooklyn to find out if there was any Draymond Wallace who had been admitted. The only answer we constantly received was that there wasn't. Because there was nothing to know or hear, I popped another Percocet, washing it down with Tequila, just to get rid of my headache and the pain from my bullet wounds. Just as I was about to take another gulp of Tequila, my mother called my name.

"Yo!" I yelled from the kitchen.

"Your father wants you."

What the fuck does he want, I thought. I took two more swigs of the clear liquor before I decided to face my father. I sat the bottle down on the kitchen table before I headed into the living room.

With a serious face, he was sitting across from my mother and had his eyes glued to the TV. Finally taking a look at me, he asked, "Did y'all come up with a plan that you couldn't complete?" He took his eyes away from me and pasted them onto my mother.

Instantly, she dropped her head.

"Muthafucka, what?" I asked, waiting for him to look my way again.

As I had expected, he took his eyes off his wife and brought them back to me.

"Ma, came up with the plan." I pointed back and forth. "*We* were the ones that went out there and pulled the trigger."

"And?" he asked, like I was a kid in trouble because of something I had done.

My mom picked her head up, staring directly at me. She was frightened by my father's temper, but I wasn't. Her look almost begged me to stop speaking and pressing the issue. Fuck that shit. I was exhausted from that nigga's mouth.

"You know what the fuck happened!" I answered him boldly.

He stood with my mom mocking his every move. "Boy, don't let me stretch you out in front of your mother for talking to me like that."

I laughed.

"You disrespecting me in my house?" He strolled towards me.

My mom tried to stand in front of him, but he pushed her out of the way like a child, forcing her back onto the sofa. She regained balance as she sprung up to her feet one more.

The closer he got, the more I was seeing red. I wasn't a child anymore and I'd be damned if he at least thought he could speak to me any kind of way he wanted. He didn't put in any work but wanted to run his fucking mouth a hundred miles per hour.

When he was close enough, I pulled my gun from my hip and pointed it dead at his forehead.

My mom held her head with both her hands, screaming, "No, Ro! No!"

I was tired of his bullshit, so I placed my finger on the trigger.

"Show me what you got!" my father said abruptly.

"Ricardo, don't listen to him, please. Just put the gun down," my mom beseeched.

"When you pull a gun out, you pull the trigger!" my father continued.

It was like that nigga *wanted* some heat.

My mind flashed back to every single incident in which he straight out challenged my manhood and made me fold. I stood there gritting my teeth, trying to will myself to squeeze the trigger and even the score with him. But for some reason my finger was stuck.

JAE

This day was Rocket's birthday, yet I hadn't stopped crying. My eyes were so heavy from all the tears I'd shed.

"Happy birthday to you. Happy birthday to you."

I had placed twenty-nine candles inside our favorite cake, which was Junior's strawberry cheesecake. Tears rained down my cheeks as I replayed one of my favorite moments with Rocket. We were in Manhattan, just walking and talking— spending time together.

"I'm a dude who loves his kids more than life itself. I'm loyal, dependable, patient, consistent, understanding and a provider. People describe me as a militant, a leader with class, but down to earth. I'm a freak when I'm with my woman. I don't do the fuck buddies or one-night-stands. I love money more than pussy, and I'm always trying to flip a dollar or two. I don't like to be the center of attention, or in a crowd of niggas. I feel like I'm that nigga, so I exude greatness. I'm cocky, but indeed confident. I vow to teach you real from the fake and protect you from the ill's the past possess. I'm here!" He embraced me before he kissed my lips.

"Rocket, I'm here." Instead of being in Manhattan on that beautiful, memorable night, I was standing beside his bed.

He had been in a coma since he had come out of the operating room, three days ago. Seeing fluids pumped into him, and a tube stuck in his mouth had my body weak. I knew I had to stay strong for our unborn child, however. Yet and still, I had faith that Rocket would pull through.

This wasn't his first time getting shot, but this was damn sure the worst, because he was hit in the same spot that he was hit before, which was his chest.

When he was sixteen, four niggas robbed him, but before they left him, they added heat to his body. The bullet missed his heart by an inch, but all them jack boys had a huge going away party, given to them by Trap, Tray and Rocket. Along with the bullet to his chest, the newer ones grazed his neck, his right shoulder, left leg and one slug hit him in his lower back, missing his spine, but came out through his stomach, hitting his intestines. Now, he has a colostomy bag attached to the bed.

"Babi, happy birthday, to you," I sang through my tears.

Mufucka's wanted him dead but they missed the target— his head. I blew the candles out before I placed the cake on the table in the room. The machines beeped and I prayed silently that God would pull him all the way out of this bullshit.

"Rocket?" I wiped the tears away as I called his name through a whisper. "Please, mi a beg yuh, nuh drop dead pan mi." I spoke in Patwha, begging him not to die on me. I touched his hand. "I need you; I can't live without you." I looked at the machine before I turned my attention back to him. “If you leave us, just look behind you because I will be on my way to be with you!”

I rubbed my stomach again. Then, I took my seat at his side as I lay my head on the bed with my right hand inside his.

CHAPTER 3
RO

Slowly, I removed my gun from my father's forehead. I knew he'd never forgive me for what I had done, so I refused to lay my head under his roof. Moving backwards, with my pistol still in my hand, I witnessed the burden ridden upon my mom's face as she stepped between my father and me. His face was unwelcoming, yet I had to let him know that he couldn't intimidate me. I would hate to have to kill him, but to save my life I wouldn't hesitate to pull the trigger over and over again.

With no shame, my mom said, "You can't stay here."

It didn't surprise me to hear those words from her. I knew she would pick him over me, any day. She carried me for nine months in her womb, but that didn't amount to her love she had for her husband. She was scared to death of him. Obviously, she didn't care about me. She would throw me away with no issue, just as she had Rocket, all because of him.

"I know that," I said as I tucked my gun at my waist. Then, I pulled my phone out of my pocket to make a phone call. Luckily, Ta'Shonda answered on the first ring for me. Without hesitating, I screamed, "Come get me, yo!" After ending the call, I moved around my so-called parents to get the fuck out of their house. Fuck my clothes. I had a few outfits at Shonda's crib that would hold me over.

For some reason, when reaching to unbolt the door, I hesitated for a moment. I decided to use that so I could address my sucka-ass parents.

"I'd rather live out in the streets with dogs than to live with snakes."

After my decree, I opened the door to feel the summer's humidity on my skin. Then, I slammed the door behind me, closing yet another chapter in my life that was a hindrance. My parents were officially dead to me.

I popped another pill, swallowing it with only the use of my own saliva while waiting on Shonda. My bullet wounds were healed, yet my body was still sore. The only thing to take the pain away were my pills. I believed that I was hooked on them now.

***

At midnight, the block was quiet. I had walked up and down the street with my hands inside my pockets, only wishing that shit was different within my life. A vehicle had turned onto my street, just before my phone went off. It was Shonda, letting me know that it was her in the car I saw.

"Do you see me? I'm standing in the middle of the street." I walked into the middle of the street, just so she could get a better view of me.

She hung up and pulled a little closer, so I could get in the car. With no time to waste, she asked, "What happened?"

"I don't want to talk about it," I said irritably. I leaned my seat back as she was pulling away.

"You don't ever want to talk about shit. Every time I ask you something, you give me, *'I don't want to talk about it'*. Ro, that shit is getting old to me!" she screamed, like I wasn't even in the car.

Shonda's fucking mouth was going to get her killed. I was still shocked that I hadn't knocked a tooth out of it just yet. Moments like these, I realized how good I had it with Red. She never bitched, complained, or nagged. *Damn!*

Boom!

I kicked the dashboard. “Shut the fuck up!” I pulled the pistol from my hip and sat it on my lap, with my eyes hard on her.

Shonda kept her eyes on the road. Instead of shutting the fuck up, she continued to exercise her gums.

I shook my head as I reached into my pocket for my pill bottle so I could pop another fucking pill. I needed to be as numb as possible around this bitch before I did something crazy to her.

CHAPTER 4
JAE

"Baby, listen. I've been doing a lot of thinking about what you desire, and I want to address the situation and give you a solution, if you so dare to accept it."

I nodded, letting Rocket know that he could continue.

"Emotionally, I can relate to the innate need to be loved unconditionally by the ones who created us. I know it hurts not being able to count on those we share the same genetic makeup with, or hear them say they love us. It's tough, but baby what can we really do? We have no power over those who don't share our view, opinions and abilities to come together when the chips are down for the moment. But that sets us apart from the rest. Instead of weakness, let's draw strength from the situation and pile all our love into each other and the kids. It's their loss. We don't need them no more. We got each other. Together, it equals family."

I soaked Rocket's bed sheets as I thought about the speech that he gave me when I told him how I was feeling without having my parents in my life.

"My solution is that we do as the bible reads and start our own tribe and love our creations the way we never were loved by our parents. Baby, put all your energy into us as a family, and as God is my witness, I'll do the same. I don't ever want you to drop another tear over them people, again. You got me and the kids to love, and we will adore you until we no longer grasp the air to breathe. Do you hear me? I don't want you to let another fucking tear escape from those pretty brown eyes over them, ever again. Our job is to love each other unconditionally so we can set

an example for the kids as your G-parents did for you. Are you with me?"

I lifted my head up as I wiped my nonstop running tears away with my left hand.

"Rocket, I'm with you. I need you to stay with us," I said aloud as if he could hear me. I pulled the tears up 'cause I knew how much he hated it when I cried.

"That shit burns my heart to see you cry," Rocket would tell me every time he saw or heard me crying.

I closed my eyes as I prayed out loud. "Lord, I'm coming to you as humble as I can be. I'm begging you to give Rocket one more chance because he's a good man, with a heart of gold. I'm asking you to bring him through this tragedy so we can move forward. I love him and I can't live without him."

I felt a small squeeze against my hand and my eyes flew open. I watched Rocket's hand move and I smiled as I looked up at the ceiling, thanking God for this beautiful sign.

"Babi, I'm here." I clutched his hand tight. I pushed the nurses' call button with my left hand.

Two nurses ran into the room, and I explained to them what had just occurred. They advised me that I had to leave the room once the doctor came in to check things out, and I went off like a bomb.

"Mi nah guh nuh weh!" I let Rocket's hand go as I stood up to face these boujee ass bitches, letting them know I wasn't going any fucking where.

One of the nurses literally ran out of the room. I repined my hair up, ready to explode.

"We'll just see what the doctor has to say," the big forehead bitch said to me.

"*I*," I hit my chest with my fist, "don't give a fuck what the doctor, security or president has to say. Mi nah guh nuh weh!"

A tall white man walked in with the nurse that left previously, with two guards following her.

"Hello, I'm Doctor Winchester," he said, extending his hand.

I was looking at him, but from my peripheral, I could see Rocket's leg moving. It prompted me to go back to my man's side to hold his hand. The doctor and nurses moved into action.

"What are his vitals?" the doctor asked while checking Rocket's blood pressure.

One nurse gave him the details while I kept thanking God over and over in my head.

"His blood pressure is one-seventeen over one-forty," the doctor announced.

"It was one-eighty over one-sixty at first, the nurse responded when checking her notepad.

Realizing that I wasn't leaving my man's side, the security guards exited the room as I moved out the way while they did their duties. The doctor pulled his sleeves up and gloved himself up.

"What's happening?" I asked as I leaned in to see what was going on.

"I'm going to remove the tube from his mouth because he's breathing on his own."

I couldn't stop the tears if I wanted to. I wore my heart on my sleeve for this man, and I wasn't afraid to express it to the world.

One of the nurses disappeared from the room, returning within a few seconds with two more white men on her tail, who were wearing gloves. When they took the oxygen tube out Rocket's mouth, I watched the lines on the screen of the heart monitor, holding my breath. A few seconds passed before the once straight lines began to move. He was still breathing on his own, and it proved that he was still alive and functioning.

Bloodclath pussyholes wanted em dead, but it nah guh end.

CHAPTER 5
RO

The second I closed Ta'Shonda's front door, I turned around and tossed the burner on the sofa, walking up behind her. Without warning, I jabbed her in the back of the head.

She spun around with her hands on her head, ready to mouth off. She couldn't. My fist connected with her mouth to shut that shit off with a quickness. Before she could scream, I punched her in the stomach as hard as I could. Shonda doubled over in pain.

The entire ride to her house, the bitch never shut the fuck up after I had already warned her.

"What the fuck, Ro?" she cried, with one hand on her mouth and the other against her stomach. When she lifted her head, blood seeped through fingers while tears swelled in her eyes.

"Keep running ya' mouth like a motor." I stood in front of her, ready to strike again if she popped off at the mouth.

She remained slumped over for a minute or so before she got herself together and ran into the bathroom. I was seconds off her ass. She spit into the toilet, and I snatched her ass up by her weave.

"This my last time telling you about your mouth."

"Ro, just let me go," she begged with tears, snot and blood was running down her face.

"Shut the fuck up and listen, dammit!" I said in her ear.

The mirror above the sink allowed me to see her face. Blood was running down her chin, onto her clothes, to the floor.

"Ya' fucking mouth gonna get you killed!" This was the first time I had ever put my hands on her like this. I swung her by her weave and left the bathroom for her to think about what I had said.

She closed the door behind me and secured the bolt. “Fuck you! Fuck you, Ro!” She yelled. “I fucking hate you!” She continued. “I hate you!” Then, she busted out wailing.

I doubled back and punched the door. “Keep that shit up and ya’ ass won’t make it out that bitch alive!” I wasn’t going to shoot her. I wanted her to shut the fuck up so the neighbors wouldn’t call the police or come to see what was going on.

That shit was out the window the momentiI thought about it.

Ding-dong! The doorbell sounded.

I walked towards the front door, rubbing my knuckles. I yanked the door open to find a big black nigga standing there. “Who the fuck is you?” I asked the nigga, grilling him the fuck down.

“Where Ta’Shonda at?”

I stared the nigga up and down, wondering what the fuck he wanted with my bitch. “What?” I asked as I reached for my gun, but it wasn’t on my hip. It was on the sofa.

Son’s eyes had zeroed on my hand, so I looked down to see what he was gazing at. I had a cut on my knuckles that was leaking. I must’ve gotten it when I punched the bathroom door. *Fuck!*

“Let her know Beam said call him ASAP,” he said and walked off.

I slammed the door and head back to the bathroom to knock Shonda’s head off her body, but the door was still locked. “You have niggas checking for you at one in the morning, now?”

I'mma beat this bitch so bad that she gonna wish she was dead, I said to myself as I kicked the bathroom door.

JAE

The doctor let me know that a nurse would be in every fifteen minutes or less to check on Rocket, even though the tubes hooked up to him were also connected outside the room to the nurses' and doctor's station.

"He needs plenty of rest," said the doctor on his way out the door.

I rolled my eyes at his statement. I didn't like these muthafuckas out here at all. They acted like I was slow or stuck on stupid. I knew my man needed rest. All I wanted to do was be by his side every step of the way.

I dialed Trap's number as I took my seat beside Rocket's bed. "Bruh, he's awake," I said after he answered.

"I'm on my way."

Then, I hit Ms. Judith's line. She answered without saying hello. She was breathing heavily as if to be expecting the worst.

"He's awake, but he's still unconscious," I informed her.

She replied excitedly, "Thank you, Jesus!"

I spent a few more minutes on the phone to update her on his conditions, and ended our conversation with, "Let OX know that he's alive."

"I will, Jae. Thank you for standing by him through everything."

"No need to thank me; it's my job."

After ending my call, I called Jamaica, knowing good and well that OX would call Gotti, so I didn't need to. JJ answered the phone.

"Wah a gwan?" I asked.

"Wi deh ya a wait pan yuh fi call back."

He said they were waiting on me to call. When the fuckery happened to Rocket, I called my baby sister, Chessan, in the back of the ambulance to let her know to tell our brothers to get ready to come to the land of the snitches— America.

She said she would be here soon.

"Unno readi fi cum up yah?" I wanted to know if they were ready to travel.

"Jae, a James wi last name, wi stay readi." JJ let me know that our last name was James and we were born ready.

"Seh unno soon den."

"Sey nuh more."

I told JJ I would see them soon and he said to say no more.

Rocket's room door opened and I moved my head to see who it was. I had my 9-millimeter on me, and I wasn't afraid to bust that bitch. I would rather do a life sentence than to have Rocket die on my watch because I was caught slipping.

Trap closed the door. I could tell that he hadn't had enough sleep. His eyes were red and half way shut. He went over to the other side of the bed, where he stood.

"You need some space?" I asked.

"If you wasn't in here, this nigga," he pointed at Rocket, "would repeat everything to you."

I smiled. Trap knew Rocket longer than me, but we loved him the same.

"Bruh, I've been in the streets, hunting." Trap took his fitted off his head, absentmindedly showing me that he had cut his dreads off. "Nigga, you almost gave me a heart attack when I heard the news from Jae, but I knew she wouldn't let you die, fam." He glanced at me and I bobbed my head. He placed his fist on Rocket's hand. "You gotta come out this shit, son. Niggas probably throwing a party right now."

Rocket's eyes opened and Trap smiled. My heart thumped with joy as Rocket's eyes closed.

"I got them extra hands on the way," I spoke to Trap as I got up from the seat. "We gonna hold him down to the fullest." I left the room to get something to drink and call Gotti.

It's show time!

ROCKET

I remembered going outside to get my phone, and then I heard the screeching tires. I tried to run back inside the house, but the slugs had me moving as slow as a snail. I know I turned the doorknob, then everything went black. I opened up my eyes, but the room was dark. I could hardly see anything. I could hear nonstop beeping noises. I tried to move my body, there was a shooting pain that made me stop and shut my eyes again.

"Aahhhh," left my mouth. My throat was sore and dry.

Someone grabbed my arm. "Babi?"

I opened my eyes and to see a silhouette standing over me underneath dim lighting.

"Babi," she said, but I couldn't respond. She let my hand go, just after I shut my eyes. I knew she wouldn't be far away.

"Mr. Wallace?" a male's voice called to me.

Reopening my eyes, I could see a man standing over me, holding a small flashlight.

"How are you feeling?"

I opened my fist and Jae's hand got in place.

The white man used his fingers to pull my eyelids open even wider, to flash the light into them. "I'll send a nurse in so they can insert a feeding tube."

"Thank you," Jae responed.

"In all my years as a doctor, I have never seen someone survive something like this."

"He's a warrior," Jae said as she squeezed my hand.

Mufuckas wanted me dead but they couldn't pull it off.

"'Bout time yuh wake up," she said. Her hair was a mess but she was still beautiful. "Babi, I'm 'bout to step back so the nurses can tend to you." She let my hand go and two nurses came forth.

I had been in the hospital for five days according to Jae. She told me about everything that had happened.

"Gotti is holding things down for you. Trap hasn't heard anything in the streets about who touched you. The girls are good, and ya' father can't wait to talk to you. Ms. Judith sends her love." A nigga was blessed to have a woman like her.

The door opened, and a smile appeared on Jae's face. She got up and kissed my lips. "I love you till the death of me."

"Bruh." Trap took her place. "My nigga, you had me scared!" I trusted that nigga and my woman with my life. "The streets is silent, but don't worry or lose sleep. Whoever did this shit gonna pay, and that's on Tray's grave!"

I closed my eyes and drifted off to sleep. Shortly after, I could hear voices again.

"You can't be too loud." I opened my eyes to see Gotti, Trap, Ms. Judith, Jae and my girls all in front of me.

"Daddy!" MooMoo ran to my left side. MiMi took the right side.

"He can't talk as of yet, so you have to do all the talking." Jae told the girls.

"I love you," MooMoo said, then MiMi followed.

I watched Jae wipe tears from, her eyes. Miss Judith expressed how happy she was to see me awake. "I can't afford to lose you and Tray, Rocket. I love you, so get well."

The girls were crying when Jae told them that it was time to go.

"I'm going to try and bring y'all up here everyday," Jae said as the girls kissed me on my forehead. "Call me as soon as you drop them off."

Ms. Judith responded to Jae, "I will and thank you."

"Miss Judith, he's my life!"

When the girls and Ma left the room, Gotti started talking. "Business is business, but I want to know what you want me to do." Trap and Jae looked at him as he spoke. "Everything is on a hold until you get better."

"What?" Jae asked as she held my hand. "I thought you was still doing business."

"I was, but OX told me to wait and find out what Rocket had in store."

Jae looked at me before she turned her attention back to Gotti. "I'm going to take over until he's better."

I squeezed her hand with all my might, but she ignored me. She knew I hated it when she was with me busting guns. Now, she was going to be by herself.

"Trap will be with me." She moved her eyes on Trap.

"I'll protect her with my life, bruh," Trap added.

"That's all I needed to know. Rocket, stay strong!" Gotti said as he hit my foot before he headed out the door.

"You." It took all my strength to get that one word out.

"Shhh." Jae placed her finger on my lips. "The streets gonna respect me because I'm you!" She bent down and kissed my lips. "So, don't worry."

"Or they gonna bow down!" Trap said, leaving the room.

CHAPTER 6
JAE

"That's not a problem, 'cause the only man I fear is God! Niggas bleed just like females." I was on the phone with Gotti. I didn't tell him that my brothers were already in the states. They were staying with Trap.

"But you are a female."

"So the fuck what! I'm not just any female. I'm Rocket's bitch." I toned my voice down a little so I wouldn't wake Rocket. "And niggas put their pants on the same way I put my thongs on. Ef a pussyhole tink seh em a guh disrespeck mi, em nah guh live fi chat 'bout it."

Gotti was getting a piece of my Patwha. I had to make it clear to him that if a nigga thought he was going to disrespect me, he wasn't going to live to talk about it.

"Well, did Rocket tell you everything?"

"With me, nothing is a secret. He showed and told me everything."

We talked a few more minutes about having one of his trusted men watch Rocket's room while I was out taking care of business. He said that he would send, Ice, his own body guard to do the job. I thanked him and ended the call.

I had so much to do, along with making an appointment to see how far along I was. I popped two vitamin E pills and one prenatal pill for the day. My stomach had a little budge, my hips were expanding and my ass had gotten to be as soft as a pillow. My finger nails were growing overnight, so I kept them filed.

Looking over at Rocket sleeping peacefully, I eased my body down into the chair so I could touch myself. It had been a minute. As my finger touched my clit, I got instantly wet. I thought about the time that Rocket fucked me in the back of the car. I had dared him that he wouldn't pull over and fuck me. Rude boy proved me wrong.

"You wanna talk all that shit, now bend the fuck over."

We were in the Casco's parking lot. He pushed my skirt up and slide my panties to the side.

"Ahh!" I screamed in pleasure holding into the door panel.

"Yea, throw me that shit, baby," he said as she gripped my ass cheeks.

"Rocket," I moaned. The car rocked from side to side as he dug deep inside of me.

"Whose pussy?" he asked, yet I didn't answer because I wanted him to use that curved dick to the fullest and punish me.

"Arhhh!" I hollered.

He pulled out and slammed back inside of me. "Whose pussy?" he asked again.

I exasperated, moving my right hand across the driver's headrest, with my left palm spread over the back window. His dick was hitting every organ inside of me and I just couldn't keep quite or hold it any longer.

My legs locked. "It's your pussy, Rocket. Yours!" I drenched my fingers with my cream.

When I opened my eyes, Rocket was looking at me with his tongue out of his mouth. I pulled my fingers out of me carefully, not to waste any of my juices on my clothes, and put them in his mouth. He closed his mouth and I came again.

Damn, I love this man.

Gotti showed up with Ice an hour later. I sized the nigga up, satisfied at what I was looking at. He was about six feet, his hooded, bloodshot eyes gave him the appearance of a convict. A deep scar wiggled like a river down the center of his nose. Lines streak. from both sides of his nose to his mouth, which he lubricates with lizard-like strokes from his tongue. His hair line was neatly shaved to form an arch above his ears. He had a low cut, trimmed haircut. I knew a killer or a pussy when I was in the presence of one. The nigga looked at me and nodded. Gotti did the introduction and I took it from there.

"Protect him with your life." I looked back Rocket. "I don't give a fuck if you tear this bitch down. Don't let nothing, even a fly, get near him."

Gotti smiled but I was dead fucking serious. Ice stared at Rocket for a moment before he faced me.

"I'll walk out this bitch with him on my back, leaving this motherfucker flat before I let anything happen to him. I got the memo loud and clear."

Ice's attitude and response was sufficient for me. He was definitely a killer.

I walked to my man's side and kissed his lips before I headed out the door with Gotti behind me. If anything was to go wrong while the watch dog, Ice, was on duty, I wouldn't spare Gotti's life.

***

I picked Trap up from his spot, leaving my brothers behind. I had to stop at each project and let them niggas know that Rocket was still the head nigga in charge, and for them not to get the game twisted.

Our first stop was Kingsborough Extension Projects. Their leader, JMoney, was in charge, but shit was always happening over there— from the money being short, to niggas disrespecting each other. Rocket let me know everything that was going on with the operation.

"You ready?" Trap asked me as I parked the 760 in the back of the building.

Niggas were outside posted up. I hit the back door and ran up the stairs with Trap behind me. I didn't stop until I was on the fifth floor. Trap was out of breath when he stopped.

"Stop blazing that ganja, bruh." I laughed, looking at him against the wall with his hands on his knees.

"Jae, you used to chase animals in Jamaica." He paused to catch his breathe. "*Bare foot.*"

"Fuck you!" I hit his shoulder in a playful manner.

We shared a laugh before I knocked on the door of the meeting spot.

JMoney answered the door with a pistol in his hand.

"The crew here?" I asked as I moved past him.

Trap told him he would close the door, so he got ahead of us and lead the way to a room full of niggas. As soon as they saw my face, they got quiet. Trap stood to the side with his pistol in his hand at his side.

"I know the rumor is out, but don't let that shit fool you." JMoney folded his arms across his chest as I shot right to the point. "Rocket is still in charge." I gaped at each nigga before I continued. "I heard the numbers were off for the last tree drop-offs. I'm not here to talk, I'm here to preach, so listen." I stopped so my words would settle in. "Let me know if I'm talking too fast, 'cuase the next time that shit happens, it won't be pretty in this bitch!" I focused on JMoney then. "You are supposed to be in charge. Either you step ya' game up, or step the fuck down; the choice is yours. Next time the shit transpires, I'm taking the head off and put another one up."

He dropped his hands and Trap aimed his .45 at his head.

"Fold them bitches, back!" Trap barked at JMoney.

He twined his arms back like he had them without a comment. Niggas were shocked with their jaws dropped.

I was a shooter, and niggas didn't know that, but they needed to know that I had a shooter around me.

"That disrespecting each other shit, cut that shit out or find another to team to eat with. We are one." I held one of my finger up. "So we should be acting like one!" A few niggas moved their heads up and down; they understood. "Don't let what's between my legs fool you." I studied the niggas in the last row. "When it comes to my man's empire, anyone can get it!" I left the crib with Trap in tow.

***

I moved around the projects in no time, letting each leader and their members know that Rocket was around and was still the HNIC. I knew niggas hated taking orders from a female, but sometimes that's just how the cards are dealt.

OX called me and said that a new shipment was on its way, so I had to make sure the money was straight. I let Trap drop me off at the hospital while he visited his mom's house to collect the bread and take it downtown to the drop-off building for me.

Ice was standing at the door when I walked in. "He woke up for a hot minute and I told him who I was. The doctors and nurses been in here every thirty minutes."

"Thanks." I moved towards the bed. Rocket was still asleep.

"Whenever, and I mean *whenever* you need a break, hit Gotti and I'll be here," he said, letting himself out.

Rocket's eyes opened and his lips curved into a huge smile. I recapped every single thing that happened to him. "I love you," he mouthed.

I smiled, showing him my missing tooth. "I love you, always!"

CHAPTER 7
RO

Hours later and Ta'Shonda emerged from the bathroom with a robe on. I had popped three pills that had me in a good daze.

"Who the fuck was that nigga?" I asked in a calm voice.

Her face was swollen but she had to deal with that, thanks to her woodpecker's mouth. "Who did he say he was?" The bitch asked me a question instead of answering my fucking question.

Not in the mood to knock her head off her body, I kicked my sneakers off and closed my eyes.

"Ro, you know all that shit was out of hand," she said when she climbed in the bed with me.

I thought about Red's death, how my mom helped me with shooting my brother, her child, and how I pulled the hammer out on my pops.

The money that the feds had given me for the last nigga was getting low and I knew I had to find someone else to snitch on so I could keep some change in my pockets and bounce from New York before it was too late.

Ta'Shonda tried to push her body against me but I pushed her off. I wasn't in the mood for no pussy.

"That's how you acting, now?" I heard the rejection in her voice when she quizzed me.

"Man, ya' mouth is off the chain, yo." I opened my eyes as I turned her around to face me.

"Ro, I don't mean to pop off at you all the time, but it seems that's the only way I can get your love and attention."

Because of the light from the TV, I could see the love she had for me in her eyes. I pulled her into my arms. I had to be careful with her; shewas my last base.

***

Ta'Shonda woke me up to some bomb ass head. For a second I was glad that I had smacked the bitch around last night. Her mouth was ugly but yet it was beautiful when she domed me out.

I grabbed the back of her head as I busted my seeds down her throat.

"How you feeling?" she asked as she sucked the head of my dick to get the last little bit of my juice.

"Good." It was the truth, but I was still wondered why she didn't tell me who the nigga was at the door last night.

I heard my phone ringing, so I pushed her from between my legs to answer the call.

"Damn, Ro!"

"Hello?" I answered, ignoring Ta'Shonda.

"Ro, how are you doing?" Chucc, my police partner asked.

"You know me." I got up off the bed, looking for my boxers.

"I have a job for you."

The news made me move faster than a track star. I was in my boxers and in the bathroom with the door shut in seconds. "Break it all down to me, Chucc!" I was excited to make this money.

ROCKET

The doctors walked in after Jaw had told me everything.

"Hello, Ms. James," one doctor addressed her. I planned to change that shit to Wallace when I was back on my feet.

"Hello," she answered in a polite tone.

"We are going to take him into the operating room to remove his feeding tube, so he can become regular on his own."

Jae smiled, but I knew if I had to rock a shit bag for the rest of my life, she would be right there beside me, emptying that bitch.

"How long will that take?" She inquired.

"A few hours," the doc replied.

"Ok." She kissed me before they wheeled me out the room.

***

When I woke up, Ice was babysitting me. I was tired, but I knew it was from all the medicines that were pumping through the IVs. My throat was just as sore as it was before. Luckily, I was able to eat ice chips and drink liquids.

"How's the team doing out there without me?" I asked him.

Ice was hesitant to answer the question, yet he did. "Great. Your lady is just like you, all the way."

I smiled inside, loving the fact that Jae was holding me down like I knew she would. She was Team Rocket till the death of her.

"She representing you like you are on a vacation." He took a seat by the door in the chair.

My mind drifted off as he continued to talk. I wanted to know who pumped those slugs into my body. There was no way Cuba could have gotten the news that quickly about his daughter unless Yellow Man had called him when we stormed the house. I knew Yellow Man's brother, Mayo, didn't know where I lived, so I erased that thought. As soon as my feet were planted on solid ground, I was going after them mufuckas.

The door open and Ice stood out the chair, ready to go ham. When seeing Jae's face, he relaxed. MooMoo and MiMi was with her. I was happy to see my little ones and my woman. Jae handed Ice a brown paper bag, then he bounced.

"I missed you," MooMoo said as she held my hand.

"Me, too," MiMi chirped in.

"How is school going?" I asked.

"Good, but I can't wait to spend the weekends with you," MiMi responded to me first. Judging by her facial expression, I could clearly see that she was upset. My daughter was saying something without telling me the details.

"What's wrong MiMi?" MooMoo asked, seeing what I saw.

The tears appeared before she answered. I tried to sit up, but the pain kept me down. MooMoo moved around to MiMi's side and held her as she cried. It fucked me up seeing my little one crying and I couldn't help.

"Tell us what's wrong, MiMi," MooMoo stated.

"Mommie said daddy was going to meet his maker, and how she wished he never came home. I told her not to say that about you and she got mad."

Damn! I shook my head as my oldest held my youngest.

"What else she said?" MooMoo asked, getting mad for me and with me.

"She beat me with her leather belt," MiMi continued. She lifted her shirt up, exposing her lower back.

I could see the belt marks clear as day. My blood pumped death for that bitch ass baby mother of mine.

"She didn't want me to go to school."

Tears ran down MooMoo's face. I knew Ashanti was stupid, but not plum stupid.

"And she said…" MiMi stopped to fix her clothes back. "If I told anyone what she said and done…" She dropped her head.

"She said what, MiMi?" Jae asked, pacing the room with her fists balled up.

My little one picked her head up and I reached my hand out to her. She walked towards me and held my hand. I wanted her to know that I was there for her even though I was laying in a hospital bed.

"What did she say, baby?" I asked.

"That she would fuck me up worse."

Jae was out the door.

"I promise you on my life, she won't aver hurt you again!"

CHAPTER 8
JAE

"I've been waiting on this day, again," I told Trap, just before I smashed the brakes in front of Ashanti's crib. "Mi tyad of dis sketal yah!" I jumped out the car, telling Trap how I was tired of the hoe.

I almost kicked the bloodclath door off the fucking hinges when she didn't answer after I knocked the third time. Trap was standing behind me. He'd seen me in action plenty times before when it came down to Rocket.

The bitch answered the door, running her fucking mouth, but I cut her off with a right jab. I backed the hoe into the house with my jaw crackers. *Bop! Bop!* I heard the front door shut and I knew Trap was inside watching the show.

Ashanti had long arms, so when she grabbed me by my ponytail, I knew I had to get the bitch up off of me. I threw a wild punch and it connected with her nose. She let my hair go, and I attacked the bitch like a wrestler. I picked her up and slammed her ass through her glass table, not thinking at the moment about my unborn child. I jumped up on my feet, so she didn't get a chance to kick me in my stomach.

"Get the fuck up and fight, bitch!" I told her, waiting on her to get on her feet. I had one of my feet in front of my body, ready to handle the hoe.

"What the fuck, Jae?" she whined, getting up slowly.

Glass was everywhere— all over the floor and her clothes. Blood was dripping from her arm.

"Mi tyad a yuh mouth."

Trap busted out laughing 'cause he knew she didn't answer Patwha, so I repeated that shit so she could understand me.

"I'm tired of your mouth, bitch!" I ran up on the hoe, fist first. I didn't want to say anything about MiMi.

Bam! Bam! I hit the bitch in her eye and nose like Rambo. She staggered back and I kept walking up on her, landing my knuckles to her face. She swung, but I blocked the shit with my left forearm, as my right hand came up and rocked that bitch in the temple. Her body dropped.

Just when I was about to tramp her ass with my foot, Trap grabbed me from behind. "That's enough, Jae," he said.

"Fuck that hoe," I returned, redoing my hair when he let me go. I fixed my clothes, ready to go for another round, but the bitch didn't get up. "Let's go, yo!"

I left the house, feeling ten times better than I've ever felt in a long time. I called Ms. Judith and explained to her what had happened. She said she was on the way to the hospital to get the girls.

***

I dropped Trap off and talked to my brothers for a few minutes.

"Ow long yuh tink seh wi a guh bi up yah?"

I laughed because TT's accent was stronger than mine. He wanted to know how long they were going to be in the states.

"Mi nuh know, but mi need unno up yah till Rocket can get back pan em foot." I needed them here with me until Rocket was able to be on his feet.

They shook their heads.

"Well mi wan fi guh seh deh city, tu." JJ, my baby brother, spoke up, saying how he wanted to see the city.

I told Trap to bless each of my brothers with some bread.

***

When I arrived at the hospital, Ice was seated outside the room. Ms. Judith was inside with the girls and Rocket.

"Jae!" MooMoo acknowledge me with joy in her eyes.

"Hey, babi." I embraced her. MiMi was in the chair, knocked out.

The right side of my face burned, so I rubbed it. That bitch Ashanti had scratched me. We talked for an hour before Ms. Judith decided that it was time to go.

"Let's go, Moo," Miss Judith said, picking MiMi up. "It's late."

Once they left, I asked Rocket how he was feeling.

"Yo, that bitch ain't shit!" I knew he was referring to Ashanti, so I sat in the chair and listened. "Ashanti trying to turn my seed against me." I watched him wipe tears from his eyes. I wanted to drive back over to that hoe's place and beat her ass some more.

Rocket loved his kids more than life, so to see my man hurting, it fucked me up.

"That shit ain't gonna happen on my watch!"

He smiled, so I changed the conversation. "How you feeling?" I asked again.

"Better." His voice was low but I heard him. "I'm ready to get home and back in the streets."

"Don't worry, you will," I said, giving him his cell phone. I wanted him to feel and know that it didn't matter that he was in the hospital, he was still the boss. "Give the orders from here until you're back on ya' feet." He was silent so I kept talking. "What the doctors saying?"

"Two weeks, Jae." He finally answered me, sounding irritated. He was crushed. He wanted to get back out there, but he knew he had to wait. I listened closely while he told me his plans.

CHAPTER 9
RO

"Have you ever heard the name, Omar Dermis before?" Chucc questioned.

"Omar Dennis?" I repeated the name trying to think if I did.

"Yes, Ricardo, Omar Dennis," Chucc confirmed.

"The nigga ain't' got no street name?" I asked as I pulled my boxers down to take a shit. The pills had my stomach fucked all the way up.

"Yeah, I think he do. Hold on!" I heard Chucc shuffling through some papers through the phone. "Hang tight, my man."

Whatever these crackers wanted me to do this time, I hope they were ready to cash out some dough, because I wasn't going for anything under $70,000.

"Ro," he called out.

"I'm here."

"Okay, his street name is JMoney."

"JMoney?" I know that name.

"Omar JMoney Dermis."

"I'ma hit you right back, Chucc." I ended the call with my mind on a damn mission.

I flushed the commode about five times while I tried my fucking hardest to think of who the fuck JMoney was. Minutes passed before I finally realized that I knew who the nigga was, thanks to his Facebook account. Omar and I went to PS161 school together. Son was a spoiled ass crybaby in class. When he couldn't figure shit out with his class work, he would whine like a little spoiled bitch. His people kept him fly in all the latest fashion, and all the females flocked around him because he stayed fresh to death.

Omar had a brother who would pick him up from school all the time in expensive cars, with a pretty chocolate bitch driving. But I remember our last year of junior high school, his brother got smoked by the NYPD in front of their mom's house for brandishing a firearm. Omar never returned to school, but I got wind years ago that the nigga was making it do what it was supposed to do in the streets. I just didn't know him as JMoney.

"Yea, I know him. He got a FB page." My voice was full of excitement when Chucc answered my phone call.

"Good," he added cheerfully.

"He still in Brooklyn I see," I said, looking at my screen to see that his Facebook location was Brooklyn, New York.

"Yes, he's running Kingsborough Projects, hard."

"Word?"

"Yea."

He was thrilled like it was the best news he heard when I said I knew who he was. I swear these crackers got a hard on when it came to me setting muthafuckas up.

"I need you to get close to him and find out who his plug or connect is."

"I can do that, but I want my money up front before I testify."

The phone got silent and I heard Ta'Shonda outside the door, so I flushed the toilet again and was careful not to say a name.

"You bring him and his connect to me and testify to make sure they don't see the light of day again. I'll make sure you get triple!"

"That's a deal!"

Money talks and bullshit walks.

JAE

"But you just now bringing this shit to my attention?" I couldn't believe that this old head, OG as he claimed to be, let some out of town nigga beat him out of $150,000 of drugs 4 days ago. "My question is though, how am I just hearing about this?"

"Boss—"

"There is no excuse!"

I was parked in front of Black E's apartment. A nigga from Wilmington Delaware, that goes by the name KB, came all the way to the city to pick up some work. I was listening to how, during the transaction, the jack boy pulled out a hammer on Black E and took everything, even the extra bread he had in his pockets.

"You know where the nigga be at?" Out of town or not, no nigga fucked with my man' s money.

"Yea, he from the Westside."

"Yuh taking me down to that bitch and point that nigga out to me."

***

I drove back to the hospital to let Rocket know what was going on.

"How you going to do this?" Rocket asked as I helped him sit up in the bed. It was hard for him to sit up on his own after the surgery. The doctors mention that he had to be in a wheel chair for six weeks before he could put pressure on his body.

"I'm going to do what you would do, babi."

"And what's that?"

"Let them niggas bow the fuck down!"

He smiled and grabbed my hand.

"Bruh?" I hit Trap's line up after I talked with Rocket. "I'm 'bout to swing through."

"Domino's or Pizza Hut?" he asked, trying to see how fast I was going to get there.

"Dem together!"

He ended the call, leaving me to kiss Rocket on his lips before I could hit the door.

"I love you," Rocket told me.

"I love you too." I left, then, about to let the nigga from Delaware know who Rocket was. He had an army, better known as me, Trap and my brothers.

***

Hours later, Trap and Black E were ahead of me and my brothers.

"Su yuh decide weh yuh a guh duh with deh otha youth?" My oldest brother, TT, asked if I had decided on what I was going to do with E as we passed a state Trooper on the highway.

I gave Gotti the story Black E had given me. He said that Black E had been with the team since day one. The only reason why he probably didn't bring the problem up was because he thought he could get the product or money back, himself.

TT shook his head after I told him the story. My other two brothers, Chris and JJ, were in the backseat listening. I told Trap before we pulled off that if that nigga Black E got on the phone at anytime, make him pull the car over and smoke that ass.

"Damn, since day one?" Chris, the second child of my father, asked.

All our father's children looked just like one another. We shared the same eyebrows, wide smile, broad nose, thick hair, and a blue-ish black mark on our left arm.

"Yea, that's what they said. When I asked OX about it, he said that Black E was as real as they came. He'd done did ten years of his life for the team."

"Loyalty is hard to come by, sis," JJ said.

"I know!"

We are suited up and ready to roll out when E pulled me to the side. "I didn't tell you because I thought I could handle the move, myself." E stared me directly in the eyes as he continued. "If I knew where the nigga's momma lived, I would've visited the bitch the day after." He paused. "I've been dealing with the nigga for two years. I never thought he would have done some shit.

"It's all good. We're here now."

I didn't know these niggas, but I was going in headfirst to what belonged to my man. Fuck these Delaware niggas. Anyone could and would get it. We were altogether on this move after leaving the other car at a Motel 6 on New Castle Avenue.

"Keep straight, down New Castle, pass the Cas Bar and we'll run into Fourth Street," Black E coached me from the second row of the Subruban. "Man, this nigga Moe Good repped this city mad hard before niggas knocked him off."

"I heard about that nigga, Moe Good," I comment. Rocket mention dude. When he was down, they were cellies. Moe Good was running the city dumb hard until niggas started hating and killed him and his sixth baby's ma, together, when he came home.

When I told Rocket about the news, he said that shit was fucked up 'cause son was a real good nigga.

"That's the house right there on the left." Black E pointed out.

I parked the truck two houses up.

"You ready, Jae?" TT asked me.

"James breed till the day I die. Let's go get em!"

***

My crew watched from the side of the house as I knocked on the front door. Trap didn't like the idea, but that was the only way in without alarming the neighborhood. I rang the bell and touched my vest under my hoodie.

"Who is it?" a nigga sounded off from inside the house, seconds later.

"Jae!"

"Who?"

"Mi car bruk dun deh street, mi need elp!" I hit my Patwha, saying how my car broke down the street and I needed help.

The door swung open and a short nigga with a Kufu on his head was staring down the barrel of my Glock 40.

"State ya' governement, son," Trap demanded the nigga with his .45 aimed at his temple as he pushed dude in the house with the hammer.

"He ain't KB," Black E said, closing the door behind my brothers.

"Ya' name what, nigga?" TT asked as he reached around me and smack the nigga with his pistol.

"My name, my name…" The nigga was stuttering. "I'm Blue," he answered in agony.

"Who else in the crib?" I added my voice.

"Just, just me." His hands were shaking as he pointed to himself and holding the left side of his head.

TT, Chris, and JJ left us as they searched the house.

"Where KB at?" I questioned as I picked a cell phone up off the couch. Black E stood at the door. I scrolled through the contact list in Blue's phone until I found KB's info.

"Man, that nigga always doing some dumb shit, yo," he said, looking at me. "I don't have shit to do with what he got going on." Tears were running down his face.

Trap tapped his temple with the gun.

"He'll be here in ten minutes," said Blue.

I checked the recent calls and saw that KB's name was there. My brothers came back in the front area, letting us know that the area was body free, but there was water boiling on the stove.

"What's up with the boiling water?" I looked at Blue.

"KB told me to have the water boiling for him." He paused and drop his head. "So he could cook up some work."

I glanced at my brothers. TT and Chris both had guns. JJ, on the other hand, had a machete.

"Oh yea," Trap said, clocking Blue upside his head again. This time, blood splashed all over Trap and Blue's white T-shirts. "You gotta suffer 'cause you associated with a traitor!" Trap was heated.

Blue's phone rang in my hand and it was KB calling.

"Answer that mufucka, and if you slip up and say something stupid, yuh dead!"

Chris hit the switch, turning off the light in the room that we were in as TT looked out the blinds.

"Yo." Blue's voice was trembling as he answered the phone. I was close enough to hear KB saying how he was about to pull up. "Aite."

"Unlock the door, too," KB told Blue before he ended the call.

Black E unlocked the door as Trap moved bloody Blue into another part of the house. TT, Chirs and JJ took different posts in the room. I sat on the sofa with my .40 on my lap. My heart raced and my finger twitched to pull the trigger. Seconds turned into minutes. Then, the knob turned.

In came a male shadow. He closed the door in the dark, not seeing Black E in the corner or any of us. "Yo, Blue!" He called out, locking the door.

TT flipped the light switch on, and the look on that nigga KB's face let me know he'd seen the end when he saw us. He dropped the duffle bag he had and tried to make a run for it, only to come face to face with Black E's hammer.

"Surprise, nigga!"

"Well, KB, let me introduce you to the party."

Trap and Blue joined us back up front. He turned around to see who I was, then looked at Blue's fucked up face.

"I'm Jael. Rocket is my man. He's not here, but the crew is present." I waved my gun around the room, looking at my army. "You already know Black E. Days ago you chose to get brave and rob the hand that was feeding you." I stood to my feet. "I'm here to collect what you took and more." I was standing in his space.

His face expressed how he wished he'd never did that shit to Black E, but it was too late for that.

I reached down and open the duffle bag to see five packages wrapped in clear plastic. The packages were stamped with our logo— CR. I pulled one of the packs out and studied it. It was a brick of cocaine. I dropped it back in the bag and zipped it up with a smile on my face. Not only was I getting back our product, I was taking their lives, too.

"Yuh a guh mek em suffa?" JJ asked me if I was going to make him suffer.

"Yuh wan fi duh deh job?" I wanted to know if he was up to do the job.

"Yea, mon."

I moved out the way as JJ went forth with the machete in his hand. He swung it forward and it took off KB's left arm completely. The nigga hollered out in pain as blood gushed over JJ and Black E.

Blocka!

I turned around to see Blue's body on the floor by Trap's feet.

Blocka! Blocka!

Trap fired two more slugs into the nigga's head. KB tried to run but JJ's machete was faster than a bullet. It took KB's head totally off his body. His head rolled to Chris' feet, and he let a round off in the head. The rest of KB's body crashed into the wall, and I let a few shots off into it. Black E's look let me know that he hadn't witnessed anything like this before. TT looked at me, and I shook my head. I had asked Rocket before I left if I should body Black E and he said no. I just hope he told me the right thing.

Trap snatched up the bag off the floor. "You ready, sis?"

I nodded as we left the house with our hoods covering our heads.

CHAPTER 10
ROCKET

The more I reflected on what Ashanti had said and done to MiMi, the more I hated the dumb bitch. I couldn't wait to check that hoe for beating my fucking daughter like she did. I knew Jae had given Ashanti the business with her hands, but that wasn't an adequate amount for me. Ashanti had enough fouls and strikes against her, altogether.

Jae and I decided that MiMi would stay with Ms. Judith until I was back on my feet. MooMoo let me know that she was okay and that her mom had sent her best wishes.

"Can I stay with Miss Judith, too?" Moo asked.

I told her she had to ask her mother permission first, so she called La'Quinnta from her cell phone, and she agreed that she could stay because it was Spring Break.

"What time is it?" I asked Ice.

He was sitting up in the chair at the door with his eyes on the TV, but his hands were in his lap, gripping his pistol. "Almost four in the morning," he answered.

I pulled my phone from beside me to see if Ashanti had called me back, but she didn't, which was cool with me. She was just making it harder for herself.

Ice stood up and fixed his jeans, tucking the gun at his side. Before he could do anything else, the door opened and I watched his hand travel to his waist for his hammer.

"Mr. Wallace, how are you feeling?" the petite nurse inquired as she made her way to my bed.

"Good." I lied. I was thinking about the Delaware trip that my baby was handling.

Ice kept his eyes on the nurse as she moved towards me. His hand never left his hip.

She checked my vitals and logged what the machine had displayed on the screen on her clipboard. "You've come a very long way," she said with a smile plastered all over her face. This bitch was flirting. "And you are still very handsome." Just like I thought

Her weave was jacked the fuck up, and on top of that, she didn't have any edges. Jae was my only type, and at the time I was worried about her trip. Ice took his seat with his head and eyes on her every move.

"Married?" she asked as she checked the fluids on my legs.

"Yea, married to me."

Ice chuckled as the nurse turned around to find Jae standing in the door way. The bitch left the door open when she came into the room, so we didn't hear Jae when she entered.

"Excuse me?"

"Bitch, you heard what the fuck I said!"

I smiled for the first time because I was fucking worried about her safety out of town.

Jae was now on the other side of my bed, cracking her fingers. "He's married!"

Ice laughed on his way out the door.

The nurse was speechless. She stepped back and got into a professional mood. "I'll let your doctor know your status." She hurried out the room, not looking back.

"Yuh gonna let me body these hungry bitches over you?" Jae leaned in for a kiss. She tasted so damn good that I didn't want to release her tongue. "Fuck around and I'll become a nurse up in this bitch," she said, pulling her lips away from mine.

I cracked a smile 'cause I knew she could do anything she put her mind to.

"You know damn well I don't want none of them bitches. I only want you," I remind

her as I squeezed her hand, all the while checking her body out.

"Oh, you better, Rocket!"

Her face was glowing, and the jeans hugged her hips like glue held paper. She watched me look her up and down as she took my hand and placed it on her stomach. It wasn't flat anymore like it used to be. She had my baby in there.

"How far are you?"

"Probably two months or more."

I closed my eyes with my hand still resting on her stomach, feeling like shit, because here she was pregnant with my child and running my empire without me beside her. She had a lot on her plate, so I asked God to watch over her and my unborn child, 'cause I didn't know what I would do if she lost the baby because she was stressed and over-worked.

"I'm fine!" she exclaimed, as if to be reading my thoughts.

I opened my eyes as she dropped my hand from her stomach.

She pulled a chair up beside my bed. Luckily, I was already sitting up.

"We handled the situation in Delaware." She pulled her hair up in a ponytail.

"We as in who?"

"When this shit took place— you being shot—I called Jamaica and invited my brothers on a vacation. Before you say something, hear me out."

I raised my hand, telling her to continue.

"I know you trust Trap with ya' life, and I trust my brothers with mine; not that I don't trust Trap; but more loyal eyes are better than four."

"And?" I asked, 'cause blood was just blood. If the loyalty ain't there, blood ain't shit.

"Babi, I know what Ro did, but my family is nothing like yours!" She defended her siblings.

"And if they turn out to be anything like mine, then what?"

"I'll pull the trigger myself!" she said so firmly that my heart skipped." Loyalty over everything, even family!" She quoted my verse to me like a scripture from the bible.

RO

Ta'Shonda was standing outside the bathroom with her hands on her hips when I opened the door. "What?" I asked, wondering how long she had been there, and what it was that she heard from my phone call. "What?" I asked again, feeling guilty.

"Nothing." She shook her head. "Why are you so uptight?"

I moved passed her and gathered my clothes from the floor. I could feel her eyes burning a hole through the back of my head. To take the heat off me, I inquired, "What do you have planned for the day?"

She just stood there, staring at me. "Huh?" She didn't blink or move.

I stood up, pulling my black tee over my head. "Ta'Shonda!" I bellowed, making her jump from fear. "You don't hear me talkin' to you, yo?"

"No, I'm sorry, baby. I was day dreaming."

"About that nigga that knocked on ya' door last night?"

"Ricardo, what the fuck ever!" She stormed out the room.

The bitch had yet to say who the fuck the nigga Beam was.

I laced my black Air Force One's on my feet, thinking of how I was going to get close the nigga JMoney without looking or acting suspicious. I then grabbed my cell phone off the bed, and headed to the living room to locate Shonda's car keys.

She was seated on the sofa with her eyes locked on her phone. As soon as I get my paper up, I was dropping this hoe out of my life for good, even though the pussy was good.

"Where ya' car keys at?"

She didn't take her eyes off the screen of her phone, yet replied, "Over there on the stand, beside the TV."

I found the keys, returning, "I'm going to get the rest of my shit from my mom's spot.

"Yea, yeah. Whatever!" was her response.

I turned around to find her eyes focusing on me. Her fucking mouth was off the fucking chain. "I see you having lose lip issues. If I was you, I'd pipe that shit down!" I opened the door, looking back at her. "Keep trying me." I slammed the door so hard, I thought the bitch came off the hinges.

***

It was 11AM and niggas were out on their grind in front of Kingsborough Projects, heavy. I parked the car a little away from the third building. My phone buzzed before I could get the key out of the ignition.

"Hello?"

"Ricardo, I'm sorry about what happened last night." It was my mama.

"Ever since I can remember, you've always put him over ya' kids. As I said last night, ya'll are dead to me!" I ended the call in my mom's ear. Fuck her and my father.

I exited the car, only to be approached by a little soldier with a purple Crown Royal bag.

"What you want?" he asked.

"Huh?"

"Pills, that white girl, hard or that boy?"

He thought I was an addict looking to buy pills, powder, crack or heroin.

"Nah, my dude. I'm looking for—"

He walked off before I could finish my sentence.

An older cat inched towards me with his hand clearly on his pistol. "Who're you lookin' for, B?" He stepped directly in my path.

I felt stupid for leaving my pistol at the crib.

"JMoney." I wave hands in the air, letting him know that I wasn't strapped.

"You got an invitation?" He pulled his hammer from his waist. Dude had scars all over his face and hands.

"Naw, I'm tryin' to link up with him on some business."

"You the police?" He pointed his gat at me.

I shook my head and my hands. "Nah, I ain't the police."

"You smell like a pig, son."

"What?"

A few more niggas joined him.

"Check his pockets, Buck!" the nigga with the gun ordered, and a nigga with four fingers on his left hand stepped up to me.

"Lift ya' hands higher, B," Buck told me.

"What, nigga?" These niggas had me fucked up if they thought they were gonna disrespect me like this.

"You heard what I said, B. Lift them muthafuckas up like you praising God!"

I found myself surrounded by a gang of them who made a circle around me.

"Yea, he the police!" The nigga with the scars all over his face and hands announced.

CHAPTER 11
JAE

"Rocket, no matter the price, the cost or the people, my loyalty is with you till the death of me."

"Babe, I'm not questioning your loyalty. It's your brother's that I'm concerned about."

I understood that Rocket had trust issues, but I needed and wanted my brothers out there with me until he was capable enough to get back to work. I would rather have them over some random stranger having my back.

"As soon as you are up and moving, they are going back to Jamaica." I was trying my best to ease his mind.

He smiled, but I knew deep down inside that he wasn't feeling the play. "I'm cool on whatever you do, Jae."

"But, what, Rocket?"

He laughed because he knew that I knew him so damn well. "No buts, babi," he mocked my Patwha.

I smiled at his silly ass. "Have you talked to your dumb ass baby's mother?" I asked, changing the conversation.

"Which one?"

We both shared a laugh, then.

"Ashanti."

"Na, I haven't talked to her or La'Quinnta."

"So, what you have planned for MiMi?"

"Spring Break is a week and a half. By then, I should be home, so they can stay with us. In the meantime, they'll be with Ms. Judith."

"If she needs help, I'll be there."

"You act like you're Superwoman."

"You ain't know, babi? I can walk, talk, bust my pistol and chew bubble gum all at the same time."

He laughed, but he knew I could. "You gonna help me to the bathroom?"

"What you think?"

ROCKET

It was my first time having a bowel movement since I had been in the hospital, so I didn't know what to expect. I watched as Jae pushed the wheel chair to my bed.

"You need me to call the nurse to come and help me?"

She cut her eyes so hard at me that my skin burned. She lowered the railing at the side of my bed, then she lifted both my feet over the edge of my bed, slowly. Pain shot up from my toes to my lower back, then up my neck.

"Arghhhh," I grunted, feeling every joint tense up.

"Just breathe. You can do this." She encouraged me as she moved beside my waist. "Babi, on the count of three, I want you to ease up so I can put your arms over my shoulder."

"Aite."

"One. Two. Tree."

I eased my body up slowly with her help. This was my first time sitting up in the bed without the bedrail for support. My body throbbed with so much pain that I wanted to say fuck it and lay my ass back down.

"You can do it, 'cause I'm here with you." My bitch was the spinal cord to my life. "On the count of three again, I'ma help you stand up." She moved the wheelchair closer to the bed.

"My legs aren't strong enough, Jae."

"How you know, Rocket?"

I didn't know, but I wasn't trying to fall on my face either.

"I got you babi," she reminded me.

On the count of three, she had me standing up with the help of her body, then carefully she sat me down in the wheelchair. All that movement had me tired and in excruciating pain.

"Just breathe, babi. You on the road to recovery."

I didn't even want to talk. I knew we had to do this shit all over again.

She wheeled me to the bathroom. "I'ma lift you up. Hold onto me so I can unstrap this shit." She was talking about the clothing the hospital had me in.

"Okay." I was sweating like someone had took a bucket of water and poured it all over me.

"You ready?"

"Yea."

She wrapped my hands around her neck and pulled me up. Once I was standing, she pulled the strap, and the paper cloth outfit fell to the side. Baby girl kicked the wheelchair and helped me sit on the toilet. Then, she moved the wheelchair to the door and sat in it.

This was my first time taking a shit in front of her.

"I know you ain't uncomfortable with this," she laughed.

"I'm never uncomfortable to do anything in your presence."

"Oh, you better not be."

"So, tell me about our empire."

I listened while she told me of how she wanted to take JMoney out of the picture completely. The nigga continued to fuck the bread up, and people were losing respect for him as a leader because they were disrespecting each other. Through it all, he wasn't correcting the problems. I nodded, mentally taking notes.

"You not saying anything, though, babi."

"I'm listening to you, Jae." Truth be told, I was taking a shit.

"Yuck! You stink!" she exclaimed, covering her nose with her shirt, but she was still sitting with me. "Anyway, Beam bringing the most money right now. He pushing the supplies like the stock market."

I knew the nigga had it in him from day one, with how he had his team in check. "Who the least project right now?"

"The one JMoney running."

"Fix it!"

"Say no more, love." Her face was still in her shirt when she replied.

We sat in silence for a few more minutes before I spoke up. "I'm done."

She reached behind me and flushed the toilet. "You gotta lean forward so I can wipe ya' ass."

I leaned over enough so she could clean me up. It hurt like hell just to bend my body, but I did it. She flushed the commode every time she wiped my ass. And as careful as she sat me down, she helped me back up and in the wheelchair. She washed her hands, then soaped a wash cloth up to wiped my face and hands.

"I love you," I let her know.

"I know, and I love you, too." She pushed me back in the room and pressed the emergency button.

A nurse ran into the room.

"Can you get us some clean sheets, please?" Jae asked nicely.

"Yes, I can," she said, looking at me, wondering what the hell I was doing in the wheelchair without a nurse.

"Thank you!" Jae was taking the sheets off the bed by the time the nurse was leaving the room.

Minutes passed before the nurse returned with the clean sheets. By then, Jae had a hospital pan with soapy water in it.

"I'ma wash you up," she whispered in my ear as the nurse sat the sheets on the bed. "Can I get another hospital gown, too? Please and thank you."

"Sure."

When the lady brought the gown back, Jae had made the bed with the clean sheets.

"Do you need any help?" the lady asked.

"Naw, I'm good."

"Okay." The nurse left the room.

Jae brushed my teeth and washed me up from head to toe in the wheelchair. When she got to each bullet wound, she kissed them softly. I watched her wipe tears away from her eyes as she catered to my needs.

"This is for all the days I forgot to tell you how truly incredible you are, and how much you mean to me," she said kissing me as she covered me up in the bed.

"You the best," I remind her.

"Till the death of me, I'll be the best to you," was the greatest comeback ever from her.

CHAPTER 12
RO

"Wake the fuck up nigga?" someone said. I felt a sharp sting across my face with his words.

I opened my eyes slowly to find about six niggas standing in front of me. My mouth was gagged, my hands were cuffed around a pole behind my back, and my feet were duct aped together straight ahead of me. My head ached from the ass whoopings they had given me out front. They stomped me until I blacked out, and here I am now.

"So, we went through ya' shit," the nigga with the scars all over his face and hands said. "And I found a lot of information about you. But don't worry, you are in good hands, now!"

I was trying to talk but my voice was muffled. I shook my head from side to side, just hoping they would hear me the fuck out first. *Fuck!*

"You working for Officer Chucc?" A voice from behind me asked.

Fuck! Fuck! Fuck, I'm dead, I thought. I kept shaking my head, praying that God would spare me. If I made it through this, I swore to become a pastor. I beat myself up for storing Chucc's number in my phone as Officer Chucc. *Shit!*

The niggas standing in front of me cleared the path as a nigga stepped forward.

"You tried to set me up, huh?" I was looking dead at JMoney, himself. "Huh, nigga?" He asked me as he kicked me in my rib.

I leaned my head back on the pole and closed my eyes, taking in the brutal pain. I bounced my feet against the tile as tears sprung to my eyes.

"What else you found out about this snitch?" JMoney inquired from the nigga to his left. He didn't recognize me from school.

"Scarface got all the info, Boss," the dude on the left informed him.

"Scar, what you found out, my nigga?" JMoney sought from Scarface, who was the nigga with all the scars over his face and hands.

"That he fucking with Ta'Shonda from Sterling Place Projects."

"Huh?" JMoney pulled his phone out of his jeans pocket.

"We searched the car he got out of and found the registration with her information on it." He stopped for a second before he carried on. "Her number was in his phone."

"My nigga, slide through the lynching spot," I heard JMoney say on the phone, before he pushed it back inside his pocket. "Where the car and phone at?"

"Finger took the car to the cut, and I demolished the phone myself, Boss," Scarface said to JMoney.

"Let me know when B gets here, and keep an eye on this clown at all times," JMoney vocalized, leaving me with his goons.

"Hear me out," I disclose, but it came out as, "*Mmmm mm mmm.*"

Scarface punched me in my right eye. "Shut the fuck up, rat!"

JAE

I was happy that Rocket alive and wasn't disabled in any kind of way. It showed us that God was truly good to us.

"What you thinkin' about, baby?" Rocket questioned.

I was sitting in a chair, looking past the TV, into space. Honestly, I was tired as fuck. "Nothing," I responded.

"You sure?" he asked.

"I'm just tired, babi." I slouched in the chair, kicking off my J's so I could rest my feet on the bottom of the bed.

"Get some rest." I could hear the concern he had for me in his voice.

"I'll sleep when I'm dead," I said, resting my eyes.

"Alright, Superwoman."

I flexed my muscles for him. We cracked up together. We were rudely interrupted by the ringing of my cell phone.

I snatched it from my pocket. "Hello?"

"Boss, we have a huge problem."

I opened my eyes. "How huge?"

"World Trade Center, huge!"

"I'm on my way!" I disconnected the call, only to hit Gotti up. "Get Ice over here, now!" I dropped the call as soon as I got the words out of my mouth.

"What's wrong?" Rocket asked with a puzzled.

"I'm not sure, but don't worry. It will be handled." I assured him. I pressed the number three on my phone, and Trap's number popped up. I hit send, putting my Jordan's back on. "Bruh get dressed and spread the news."

"Aite. "

"I'm on my way!" I started lacing my sneaks up.

"Baby, who called you?" Rocket asked.

"Get some rest!" I said, kissing him on his lips.

The door opened, and I turned to find two white males dressed like detectives looking at us.

"Mr. Wallace, this is my partner Bromwick." He pointed to the man beside him. "I'm Wales. We are detectives from the Seventy-First Precinct."

"Go take care of the house. I got this!" Rocket said, looking at me.

"You sure? 'Cause that shit can wait, or yuh wan mi fi get demyah bloodclath out yah?"

Rocket laughed but I was drop dead serious. I wanted to know if he needed me to put these cock suckers out. Detectives or not, when it came to my man, the president could get touched.

"Naw you good, babi."

I've hated the fucking police system since they locked my uncle up in Jamaica for cutting a man's arm off completely, for stealing his ganja when I was a little girl. "Bloodclath babiland fi bun!" I mean mugged them crackers on my way out the door.

I called Gotti and told him that Rocket had unwanted visitors. So, he needed to let Ice know that the spot was hot. Ice needed to be clean, or just wait it out.

ROCKET

"How are you feeling, Mr. Wallace?" Wales asked me as Bromwick looked around the room.

"You shouldn't be asking how I'm doing. My condition explains itself," I spat. Then, I lifted the head of the bed, using the controller on the rail of it.

"You right," Bromwick chirped in.

"But you could've been dead," Wales added.

"And if I didn't make it, y'all job would've been easier!" I was getting angry.

These pussies didn't know who I was at all; coming to me like I was a sucka. They came at me like I was supposed to scared of death. If it was my time, then it was my time. Until then, I was going to let the streets bow down to my gangsta.

"We would still have to investigate ya' homicide," Bromwick chuckled.

"You wouldn't have to do all of that, 'cause one less nigga in the world is a blessing for ya'!" I reached for the cup of ice beside my bed on the food tray. "Cut the bullshit and get to the point. A nigga needs his rest."

Bromwick exited the room like I was supposed to give a damn. Fuck outta here. He was one less cracker around me. These mufuckas just got here to see if I knew anything about what happened to me. At that moment, I didn't know who pulled the trigger, I planned on finding out.

"Do you have an idea about who would want you dead?"

"And you think if I did, I would spill my guts?"

Wales crossed his arms and stared dead at me. "It's about ya' safety, not about snitching." He responded in a low tone.

"I'ma handle the shit the same way they, whoever, felt about me!" I threw the paper cup of ice across the room.

He dropped his arms at his side. "Sorry to upset you, Mr. Wallace. All I'm trying to do is help."

"You can help ya' ass out the door!" I hit the bed remote so I could lay down.

"If you change ya' mind—"

"Get the fuck out!" I sat straight the fuck up in the bed, feeling my wounds ripping apart through the staples. "Argghhh!" I inhale. "And don't come the fuck back." I lowered my body back onto the bed as the cracker exited my room.

No snitching should've been one of the ten commandments.

CHAPTER 13
RO

After JMoney left the room, his goons took turns beating the life out of me. My eyes were swollen but I could still see a little. A few of my teeth were knocked the fuck out and I had to swallow them. Blood dripped from my nose, and I wished they would just go ahead and finish me.

"What's the nigga's name?"

"Ricardo Johnson, right, Scar?"

"Yea, that's what that nigga's driver's license stated."

There were three different niggas talking; one of them were Scarface, fasho. I closed my eyes and asked God to forgive me for all of my sins that I've committed. My time was here.

Wham!

Someone kicked me in my shin. "I'm back nigga!"

I opened my eyes the most I could. I saw JMoney, Scarface and Beam. *No that could not be*, I said to myself, looking at the other nigga.

"Yo!" the other nigga shouted as he pushed JMoney's arm. "That's the nigga that answered my sister's door last night."

"Huh?" JMoney turned to face Beam.

"Last night, around twelve forty-five, Shelly, the bitch that lives across the hall from Ta'Shonda, called me saying how she heard a lot of commotion coming from Shonda's crib, so I get the fuck outta some pussy to see what's going on. I'm blowing my sister's phone up, but she not answering. So, I get dressed and race to her spot. I got a key to her crib, but I respect her space and privacy. So, I knock on the door, but she doesn't answer. I rang the bell, and this clown answers the door." Beam points down at me.

"What?" JMoney laughed.

"Oh, this shit gets better, though." Beam stops to answer his phone. "I'ma hit you right back, lil' mama." He ended the call and picked up where he left off. "Anyway, I tell the nigga to tell Shonda to hit me up, but she didn't until about two hours ago."

"Saying what?" JMoney rubbed his face with a confused look on it.

"She said how she heard—" He stopped and pressed a button on his phone. "I'ma let her tell you." Beam got the call on speaker. Ta' Shonda answered on the second ring. "Sis, tell me what you heard that nigga talking about in the bathroom."

"Why? What's up?"

"I'ma tell you after."

"Oh, lord. He said that he wanted his money up front before he testified. And I guessed whoever he was talking to said what he wanted to hear 'cause he said it was a deal."

JMoney shook his head with his pistol in his hand, staring right at me.

"Now tell me why, Beam."

That bitch was listening to me.

"I got ya' car. I'ma slide through and we gonna talk."

"How the hell you got my car when Ro got it?" Her whole tone changed.

"Don't worry, sis. I got you!" Beam ended the call.

"Finger," JMoney hollered. The nigga with the missing finger came forth. "Take Beam to his people's car."

"Aite," Finger said, walking off.

"My nigga." JMoney daps Beam up. "Nice look!"

"Son, you already know. Crown Heights till the death of us!"

JAE

Chris answered the door with a Mac 11 in his hand. "Wah a gwan, sis?"

"Mi nuh know yet. One a deh rude boi call mi an seh ow em ave ah emergency," I said, moving past him into the house.

TT and JJ were smoking a blunt with each other.

"Jae, wah a gwan?" JJ asked.

I told him exactly what I had told Chris at the door. One of the leaders of the projects called me and said that he had an emergency, but I didn't know shit else.

Trap joined us, ready to roll, dressed in all black. "You plan to get dirty in all white?" Trap questioned me.

"When you know me to give a fuck about clothes?"

TT and JJ busted out laughing. Them muthafuckas were as high as a kite.

"Never!" Trap responded with a smile on his face.

JJ and I rode together, leaving Chris and TT were with Trap behind me.

"How our grandparents?" I turned the music down as I inquired about the ones that raised me.

"Dem good! When last yuh chat to daddy?" JJ grilled me.

"Long, long, long time."

"Yuh know seh em ask bout yuh all deh time." JJ let me know that our father asked about me all the I time. Then, he wanted me to hear what our father had to say, and if I didn't want to hear what he had to say, to move on.

"Mi ear yuh." I let him know I heard him, but right now, Wilber, our father, was not my problem.

I turned the system back up, listening to *Top Shotter* by DMX, Sean Paul and Mr. Vegas.

***

"Yo, I'm out back!" I had parked the car in the back of the building. Trap and them were parked beside me.

"I'm coming out, right now," the nigga responded into the phone.

I leaned my head against the headrest and rubbed my belly. I felt JJ's eyes on me. I turned my head, and as I thought and felt, JJ was looking at my hand on my stomach.

"Yuh pregnant?" he asked, looking dead into my eyes.

"Yea." I smiled.

"How far?"

"I'm not sure."

The windows were up, so I knew Trap, TT and Chris couldn't hear me. I had planned on telling everyone when Rocket had gotten home. I saw JJ pulled his hammer from between his feet, and I ducked my head.

"Aye, aye!" I heard someone yelling. I picked my head up to find one of my project leaders with his hands raised outside my car.

"He good money, bruh!" I pushed JJ's gun down slowly and let the window down.

"Man," he said, breathing hard like he'd run a marathon. "Damn." He wiped his forehead with his hand. "Uhmm."

"Nigga, if you that scared of death, join a church!" JJ voiced.

Son couldn't even talk, so I shook my head, laughing like hell in the inside.

"We gotta ride out," he finally said, "so, I can show and explain it all to you."

"Aite, get in the back."

Son opened the back door, but JJ stopped him from entering.

"Nah, you gonna ride up front." JJ got out from shot gun and move behind the passenger's seat with his toy in his hand.

"Nah guh let nuh pussyhole catch mi and yuh bloodcloth slippin'!" I truly loved and appreciated our language, because we were talking about son and he didn't have a clue. JJ made it clear that he couldn't afford to be caught slipping by a fucking pussy ass nigga.

Son's first impression was straight pussy.

"Yea, mon." I said, pulling off.

ROCKET

Mufuckin' suckas came marching up in here like a nigga supposed to just tap out and sing the national anthem to them. Not even with my toes up could they get a word from me.

I pressed the nurses' button, and before I sat it down, in comes shorty that was trying to flirt with me with a huge ass Kool-Aid smile on her face.

"So your killer left, huh?" she asked, rubbing my left foot.

"She ain't ever far."

She moved her hand away like I told her I had HIV.

"And that ain't what you want."

She looked around the room, satisfied when not seeing Jae. "You right, I don't do pussy. I do dick, all day, everyday!"

I laughed at the bitch.

"Let me introduce myself, Mr. Wallace. I'm Kimberly." She showed me her name tag. "So how may I help you?" She circled her tongue around her lips. A thirsty bitch for sure. She left the door opened like last time, not learning from her mistake.

"All I want is a cup of ice."

"You thirsty?" She smirked at me. "'Cause if you are, I can drench you."

Ice entered the room as quiet as a mouse. He nodded at me, and I returned it.

"Is that a yes?" Kimberly asked.

"A yes to a cup of ice."

"You are no fun."

"You." She literally jumped in the air when ICE spoke. "You right. He can't be any fun with a killer in his life as a wife!"

"Whatever!" she said, leaving the room.

We shared a laugh at her expense.

"I seen them people paid you a visit," Ice said.

"Yea, but I shut them the fuck down."

"Oh, I already know you G'd the fuck up like ya' pops."

Real recognize real from a mile away, for real. I watched as he pulled the heater from his waist and tucked it under his oversized black T-shirt. I reached for my cell phone and dialed Ashanti's number again. The bitch picked up just when I was about to disconnect the call.

"So, you allow ya' little island girlfriend to just beat ya' baby ma's ass all the time, huh?"

"Ashanti, at least you lucky it ain't me beating yo' ass."

"Rocket, fuck you! And where my child at?" She yelled.

I ignored her first statement. Bitch couldn't even ride my pinky to save her life. "That's what I called to talk about."

"What?"

I know I've got to play this hoe's game or I won't see my child. "How about I keep her for a while so I can build back up our relationship?"

"Nigga, is you crazy!"

I closed my eyes, fighting the shooting pain mentally, along with this bitch's mouth. "Naw, yo, I'm serious." Holding my tongue from not going off on this hoe is hard.

"Where MiMi at?"

"She good."

"Oh, she with ya' girlfriend?" I heard the resentment in her voice.

"Ashanti, just think about it and call me back, please."

"Whatever!" She ended the call in my face.

Ice was watching TV, but knew he was listening to my conversation. I asked him to step outside so I could make another call. He agreed and exited the room with his heater at his side.

"Junior, what's crackin' with you?" My old man answered his phone.

"Healing, but ready to step back out."

"I hear you. Just be careful. Hold on, the COs making a round."

Even though OX was locked the fuck up, my father was still a boss nigga. He continued to support the streets of Crown Heights with the best drugs from his personal cellphone, from his cell.

"Aite, I'm back," he whispered.

"You straight?" I didn't want him to get caught.

"You already know I'm G'd up from the floor up. Just gotta stay on point." He laughed before he pressed on. "How the business looking?" He got serious when it came to the paper.

"Everything going excellent!"

"I like hearing that." The toilet in the background flushed. "Have you heard who was responsible for ya' shooting?"

"Naw, the streets is silent."

"Don't worry. The streets won't stay silent forever!"

I couldn't wait to find out who pumped those slugs in me.

"Son," he whispered again.

"Yea?"

"They recounting us. I'ma hit you later." He said that shit so fast and ended the call that I hardly understood what he'd said.

I called Ms. Judith to see how my little ones were doing, but they were out blowing money. She told me they would be up to see me later. I was blessed to have her in my life.

Just as I was about to text Jae, Kimberly entered my room with Ice on her heels. "You need anything else?" She handed me the cup of ice and winks at me with her fake lashes.

"My meal for the day." I laid the phone down on the bed beside me.

Ice took his seat. Within the blink of an eye, he pulled his gun from his waist and hid it under his shirt without Kimberly seeing him do it.

"Is that all I can get you?"

I closed my eyes, thinking about my woman and my child's safety while ignoring this thirsty bitch's remark. A few seconds passed before she exited the room.

"Bitch gonna fuck around and end up leaking by Jae," Ice said.

"I see it happening, too." I reopened my eyes. "Can't say I never warned her!"

CHAPTER 14
RO

I was hearing a lot of voices, but I couldn't understand what they were saying. They were so far away. I tried to move my arms, but they were so secure that it was hard to do so. I was so weak that I couldn't even lift my legs up off the tile.

"So, what you think I should do about the situation, since the police are involved?"

The voices were getting closer, yet I couldn't make out who they belonged to.

"You not saying anything?" That was JMoney's voice, but I could only wonder who he was speaking to.

"Shhh." Someone else quieted him.

Then, I could clearly hear footsteps from behind me. I opened my eyes to see three faces that I had never seen before, since I had been there. JMoney's face appears, with Scarface's next. I closed my eyes, waiting for them to strike again. After a moment of waiting, I opened my eyes to see the devil himself.

Fuck!

JAE

Out of all the people in the world, I was surprised to be looking down at Ro. Our eyes locked. I squatted directly in front of him to get a better look. He was badly beaten. Purposely, I reached back with my fist and added my touch of pain to his face.

Wham!

I caught him right up under his nose. I felt and heard the sound of bones cracking. His face turned, but I snatched him by the mouth guard, bringing his head back around. Blood trickled out his nose. I reached back one more time and connected my knuckles with his eardrum. I watched as he closed his eyes and mumble something I can't understand.

"I got it from here, yo." I was on my feet, looking back at JMoney.

"You sure?" he asked.

I no longer needed his assistance. He'd disclosed all the information I needed during the six-minute ride on the way over here, except for Ro's name. He kept referring to him as "that nigga". I damn sure didn't need all these unwanted eyes around at what was about to happen.

"Let that be the last fucking time you question my order!" I stepped inside his space to remind him of my authority.

He nodded. "Aite, y'all, let's go," he ordered his crew.

I watched as they cleared out the room. Once the door to the basement was shut, I told Trap to remove the gag.

"This is Rocket's brother, Ro. He's blood like y'all are my blood." I spoke to each of my brothers. Their faces were on Ro. "Rocket invited him and his bitch, Red, to eat at our table, and they were eating real fucking good, too."

A chair was to the side, against the wall, so I walked towards it so I could sit down and continue my speech.

I pointed at Ro like he had pointed out Rocket in court. "But he and his dead bitch Red got jammed up and couldn't bear the thought of doing time." I stopped just to see that all my brothers' faces were serious. They were waiting on me to say the word to end Ro's life. "Ro decided to tell Rocket how he would snitch on the plug instead of manning the fuck up."

Ro dropped his head.

I leaned my head back on the wall, looking at the live snake in front of me. "Rocket's motto from the gate was loyalty over everything, so he cleared the fuck out when this nigga said that he was going to fold."

Trap released the gig on the floor and stepped out the way with a smile on his face.

"Rocket warned his blood to do the right thing, but when Rocket saw that Ro's mind was made up, he took shit into his own hands. Rocket tried to erase this bitch altogether, but the bitch lived and testified on Rocket, sending him away for three years!"

Silence.

"Damn!" was JJ's remark as he looked back at me, breaking the silence.

"Trap, thank you for smoking that fat bitch, Red."

Ro lifted his head up, looking at Trap.

"It was my pleasure, Sir!" he said to Ro. The look on Trap's face was priceless. He would do it all over again if he had to.

Tears ran down Ro's face like an over flowing river. Muthafucka was hurting.

"Pain for pain. You sentenced my man, your blood, to three years!" I was getting mad all over again. I stood to my feet to go back over to him.

Ro coughed up blood.

"You didn't hear what Rocket was saying when he said man up!"

Silence again.

The smell of fresh blood made my heart beat like a trigger waiting to be finger fucked.

"I know who shot—" He swallowed a packet of blood. "I know who shot Rocket." He closed his swollen eyes for a moment before he stared back up at me.

"Who?" Trap asked, cocking the hammer back on his gun.

Ro let his head fall, but I wanted answers.

"Who, mufucka?" The bass in my tone caused Ro's body to jump.

"Our mother and my father," he confessed.

My heart stopped beating as my knees buckled under me. I had to reach out and grab a hold of JJ and Chris for support. I knew Ro's father hated Rocket, but for their mom to try to kill her son was a different type of hate.

"How you know?" JJ asked, holding me up by himself.

"I was with them!"

I believed him, just like when he told Rocket that he was going to snitch. He had the same look on his face. They all hated Rocket, so why not plot his demise together? I wasn't in Rocket's for only information. Anyone who thought they could wipe my man off this planet had it coming from me.

RO

Damn right, I told on my mother. That bitch played her part. I lied on my father 'cause he couldn't stand seeing Rocket growing up, knowing that Rocket's father, OX, killed his brother. He wanted Rocket dead just as bad as I did, so he was guilty, too.

The Jae and Rocket that I knew wouldn't let my parents live, and I was at peace with that. I knew my life was gonna be cut short for all the foul shit I had said and pulled, but I didn't know it would end like this.

Trap had gagged my mouth back, so my screams wouldn't be heard. I tried to wiggle, but they held my legs down as JJ snatched my jeans and boxers off me, exposing my dick. The tile was as cold as ice, and so was their hearts towards me.

"JJ, yuh got that?" Jae asked her brother with a devilish laugh. The bitch was the devil, himself, I swear.

"Yea, mon!" He moved from in front of me, only to return with a machete.

I tried to beg them to spare my life, but they couldn't comprehend what I was saying. It wasn't like they gave a fuck and was going to stop. They were on a mission, and God himself couldn't save me.

"Wi a guh duh em ow em duh deh batti bois a yard!"

I could never understand that shit when Jae spoke it, but I knew what batti boys stood for. Faggots.

Tears ran down my face like never before. I closed my eyes, not wanting to see what they had planned for me. Instead, I asked God for forgiveness.

JAE

I wanted this snitching ass nigga to suffer a vicious death, so I explained it to my brothers that I needed them to help me do him how they did the faggots in Jamaica back in the days.

Trap took a few steps back as JJ swung the machete, hitting its mark. Ro's limp dick. His eyes flew open as his dick hit the title. Blood spirted all over the place. Ro's head bounced back and forth against the pole. He was in major pain.

"That's how I felt when you took Rocket from me." I grabbed the machete from JJ and cut the rope that was holding his hands together behind him. "You gonna suffer like I did." I went to sleep plenty nights, crying and missing the fuck out of Rocket.

Ro tired his hardest to crawl, but I sliced his left wrist completely off. Blood hit my grey sneakers, but I kept going. I swung the machete again, taking off the hand that he held up in court towards my man.

"Take the gag out of his mouth."

TT stood on Ro's feet. Trap stood on one forearm, and Chris stood on the other with his black Timberland boots. JJ untied the piece from around Ro's mouth. I looked at the snitching bitch and smiled. I was raised to do this shit for real, and I was grateful that my G-Pops took the time out to teach me how to kill animals, 'cause that shit damn sure came in handy. I was about to do him real dirty for how he did my heart— Rocket.

Blood poured from Ro's body, but his heart was still beating. I pulled the black gloves from JJ's pocket and stuffed my hands inside them. Then, I forced my left hand in Ro's mouth for his tongue, and pulled it out as far as I could.

His eyes opened. He screamed for help, but I wasn't going to let that affect me.

I jammed the machete under his chin, slicing him all the way down to his chest. Blood splashed all over my clothes, my face and in my hair. His body struggled to stay alive, and that made me slaughter his ass more. Snitches get more than just stitches with me when you're fucking with my loved ones.

"Damn!" Trap shouted in amazement.

I added more pressure to the handle as I dug deeper with the machete. I smelled fresh shit and I knew that he had a bowel movement. I pulled the machete up, using the very tip to remove his tongue from his mouth. I dropped it beside his head once it was detached.

His eyes were fighting to stay open.

I held the handle of the machete with both hands and came down with it in his heart. I twisted it around and around. His body twitched for seconds before it finally stopped moving altogether. Afterward, I removed the blade from his chest. TT, JJ and Chris stepped back, looking at my artwork. If my grandpa was around me now, he would've given me an A plus.

"Damn!" Trap said, looking at me.

"Loyalty over everything!" I reiterated.

We got some trash bags and bleach from JMoney so we could dispose the body and clean up all the blood. Once the body was int the bag and the place was clean, we headed out, leaving JMoney behind.

I drove straight to Trap's crib with Ro's body in the trunk. "Babi," I spoke when Rocket answered his phone.

"You alright?"

"Always." I was taking off my bloody clothes in the bathroom while I talked to him. "How you feeling?" I asked.

"Happy to hear ya' voice."

"Same here."

He let me know that he'd pissed the detectives off real bad when they started questioning him. I laughed while listening to my man keeping it all the way real.

"I love you!"

"I'll be there soon. I have one more stop to make. I love you, too."

I took a shower and changed into one of my brothers' outfits. We spent the rest of the evening eating and talking while they rolled blunt after blunt. Once darkness had taken over, I drove the car to Ro's parents' house and dumped his body on their steps with the help of my family.

CHAPTER 15
ROCKET

When Jae showed up with Trap, I knew from the frown on her face something was mad foul. Ice left the room, saluting me. I watched Jae closely. She held my stare with a look of disgust and anger on her beautiful face. Slowly, she took a seat beside me.

"What's wrong?" I sat up in the bed, ignoring the pain that was shooting through my body a hundred miles per seconds. "Jae." I barked, reaching my hand out to touch her leg.

She lifted her head, just as Trap took a seat in Ice's usual chair with his head bowed.

When I talked with her earlier she sounded just fine. Her eyes were bloodshot, her fists were balled up, and her right leg was shaking uncontrollably.

Yeah, Island Gurl is heated.

"Bruh?" I looked to Trap, whose head was still low. "Give it to me raw." I removed my hand from Jae's leg.

He looked over at Jae while I my eyes were darting between the two, waiting for someone to tell me something.

"We know who shot you." Jae spoke through pursed lips.

"So, why are you all frowned up?" inquired.

"'Cause it was your blood!" Trap shouted, placing his gun on his lap.

"My blood?" I questioned, staring a hole into Jae's face.

"Yea, babi." She licked her lips before she continued. "Ro, his father—" She paused with tears returning even harder than before. "And ya' mom."

I leaned back in my bed, soaking up the news. I knew they all hated me, so it didn't surprise me. What I wanted to know was how they found out. "Who told y'all?" I lifted the bed up using the remote so I could sit up.

"When I got the call from JMoney about an emergency, I thought I had to go over there and toe tag that nigga, so I picked Trap and my brothers up." Her tears had dried up. She knew how bad I hated to see her cry. I knew my mom's involvement had something to do with her tears. "I get to JMoney's stomping ground— add on that the nigga takes me on a six minute ride to a place he calls the Lynching Spot."

I nodded, letting her know that she could keep going.

"On the ride to the Lynching Spot, JMoney is telling me how a nigga pulled up to the projects. When one of the little niggas from JMoney's crew approached dude to see if he wanted some work, the nigga turned the little nigga down."

"Okay." I was getting impatient, but I didn't let it show.

"This alarms JMoney's right hand man, Scarface, so he steps towards the nigga to see what's up, 'cause Scarface was watching the situation from when the nigga pulled up."

"Who is the nigga?" I shrugged.

Jae took a deep breath before she answered me. "Ro."

I felt my body tense up as the room got quiet. "Ro?" I asked to make sure I heard her correctly.

"Yes. The snitch that told on you."

"And?" I looked to Trap to find a smile on his face that I couldn't read.

"The nigga was fucking with Beam's sister," he informed me.

I shook my head, realizing how close this nigga was to me and I didn't fucking know. I guessed that the look on my face gave me away.

"Listen," Jae said. "You have nothing to worry about. Anyway, Ro had a fight with Beam's sister."

When Jae had told me how Ro got caught up, it didn't surprise me that the nigga was still selling his fucking soul to the police. Once a snitch, always a snitch.

"So, I'm in front of the nigga. He's beaten to the point that he's black and blue, but I don't give a fuck. I cleared the room. JMoney's niggas didn't need to know that you were related to a bitch ass nigga. Plus, less eyes are always better."

I truly appreciate Jae doing that, but that shit didn't matter to me. I was born from a real sack of nuts, and not even death could change my character.

"Bruh." Trap finally decided to talk. "Jae smoked that nigga like they did snitches back in the day." He was a little too excited.

"Word?" I glow inside, just looking at my bad bitch.

"They all helped me though," Jae added, looking over at Trap.

"Son, all her brother JJ did was cut the nigga's dick off. She did the rest." Trap had no problem with telling me how Jae killed Ro.

"I dumped his body on ya' mom's steps! Fuck that bitch. She's next on my list."

"Jae." My eyes were hard on her. "I wanna send that bitch and her husband on their way."

Her face dropped as sadness covered it. Trap chuckled.

"But y'all will be there to help me make them mufuckas suffer, right?"

Finally, she smiled again. I would die to make her happy. "You know I'ma help you make them bloodclath pussies bow down to you, Boss!"

I could feel the love she had for me in her statement. Her body was hers, but her soul was mine.

JAE

It had been a week since Rocket's mother discovered her snitching ass son's body on her doorstep. Rocket and I watched the news together with smiles on our faces. Betrayal is worst than death. Every dog got his day coming, and I was more than happy to have gotten Ro out of here, gangsta style.

The operation was running smoothly. JMoney even had corrected the money that he was short on. The nigga knew that I wasn't the typical bitch. I was glad that he figured it out because I wasn't afraid to black bag his ass, or whomever else on the team that didn't like my layout.

As always, from day one, Beam made sure that his projects collected the most work to distribute. Son tried to question me one day when I was checking on the projects.

"I heard you handled that situation."

Even though I knew what situation he was talking about, I wanted him to say it himself. "What?"

"The nigga that was fucking with my sister."

"What nigga?" I continued to play slow.

"Dude that was in the Lynching Spot."

"I don't know what you talking about," I said with a frown. Lose lips had a way of sinking ships, so I knew what I had to do for sure.

When he realized that I wasn't coming up off any information, he spat, "You're so damn smart."

I didn't comment. I just left him standing where I met him.

Ms. Judith made sure to bring the girls up there every other day to see their father. I would always watch from the shadow while they bonded. No matter how hard or gangsta he was, he had a soft spot for his little queens in the making.

My stomach was growing as the days passed, and I couldn't wait to visit the doctor. My brothers hadn't left for Jamaica. Since they were enjoying their stay, I let them move into my basement, giving trap back his space. My sister Chessan was finally in the states now, in Brooklyn, staying at my house also. These days, I was bouncing between the house, the streets and to Rocket's side.

"Ow yuh duh it?" Chessan asked me how I did it while we were eating dinner as a family, without Rocket and Trap. I didn't keep anything away from her. She knew it all.

My sister had cooked oxtails with butter beans, curry chicken feet, and white rice for tonight. TT laughed at her comment.

I rolled my eyes at him.

"Yuh pregnant and still yuh nuh tired."

I had told them all that I was pregnant. The only people that didn't know was Trap, the girls, Ms. Judith and OX. I wanted Rocket to bless them with the news. Even though I was pregnant, I knew I had a man that I couldn't let down, so I force the word tired out of my vocabulary altogether.

"Naw, mi nuh tired!" I said, getting up after I had cleaned my plate. I had to be at Rocket's side.

CHAPTER 16
ROCKET

I was finally getting out of the hospital today, and I couldn't wait. I could stand on my own, but I had to be wheeled around 'cause my body's strength wasn't where it needed to be just yet.

"You ready?" Jae asked as Trap wheeled the chair towards me.

"You know I am!"

"Trap, I gotta go get the car up front, so we don't have to push him far."

"Aite," he responded.

I was glad that Jae had left me with Trap. It had been a minute since we had some quality brother time together. "Yo, I need a favor," I said to him while draping my arm around his neck.

"What's that son?"

I knew I could depend on this nigga to come through for me, so I explained to him what I needed done, like ASAP.

"Nigga, you ain't said shit. I'm on it!" he exclaimed with a smile.

The room door opened and the nigga almost dropped me just to pull his gun out.

"You going to leave and not say good bye?" Kimberly asked, ignoring Trap's gun pointed at her.

"Tuck that shit my nigga," I whispered. "She one of the nurse that they assigned to my room." My feet were about to give out from under me from standing on them this long.

Trap tucked the gun as Kimberly ran over to us, helping me get into the chair.

"Yea, whatever, nigga!" Trap said, being smart. I knew he was thinking some crazy shit, but it wasn't like that at all with any bitch.

"So, when were you going to tell me you were leaving?" Kimberly asked me with her hands on her hips.

Trap stood back, surveying her like she was crazy, but she never took her eyes off me.

I got comfortable in the wheelchair. "Was I supposed to?"

"Yea." She rolled her eyes and snapped her fingers.

Jae never did shit like that to me. She only did it when she was checking a bitch. Trap laughed and I had to mug him for it. He was igging this stupid hoe when thinking the shit was funny.

"Listen, yo." I placed my left foot on the holder of the wheelchair. "I don't know what kind of obsession you have with me—"

The hoe put her hand up, cutting me off. "It ain't like that. I just like you, that's all."

Trap couldn't contain himself from laughing. This shit wasn't funny.

"Really, son?" I questioned him.

"You know why I'm laughing, fam," he said.

It took me back to the time that nigga had got caught up in some crazy's gut, and I couldn't stop laughing at him. We were about fourteen years old and feeling ourselves to the fullest. Out of the three of us, Tray, Trap and myself, Trap was getting more pussy than a gynecologist did in a week. We were attending a house party in the Heights one weekend when Trap met this older woman. Shorty was bad for her age to be double ours. Trap's talk game was corny as fuck back then, but it didn't matter 'cause he was dicking the old head down almost every day after school. That was until one day he was hitting it, and out came a rubber with nut out of her pussy.

"What you did?" Tray asked when Trap was telling us the story.

"Man, I pulled that shit out and kept fucking her!"

"What?" I punched the nigga on his arm.

"And that rubber wasn't mine 'cause I always flushed my shit just to make sure a bitch don't get a turkey baster and push that shit back up in her." That nigga was schooling both Tray and myself.

"So, what you did after you nut?"

"I got up and told her what we have is over. The bitch tried to say that was my condom and I was the only nigga that was hitting it."

Days passed by before shit got real bad for Trap. The old bitch found out where he lived and showed up, but instead of one of us answering the door, Ms. Judith did. We were in the living room, playing the game when we heard Ma yelling at the top of her lungs for Trap. Whenever she called one of us, we all would show up.

When we got to the front door and saw the old bitch, Trap took off running up the stairs to our room. That bitch wanted that young dick real bad. Ms. Judith cussed her ass out and threatened to press charges against her. She left and never showed back up, but Trap got chewed out by Ma for days for fucking women who wasn't his age. The old woman scared Trap straight, and he never fucked another woman five years older or younger than he was. Me and Tray clowned him for days for running away from the old head.

"Draymond, are you listening to me?" Kimberly asked, bringing me back.

"Naw," I said, laughing, but I was laughing about Trap running up the stairs to at a time, scared to death.

"I wanna fuck with you!"

"I'm good, yo." I looked at Trap and nodded my head towards the door, letting him know I was ready to get the fuck up out of here. Fuck what this thirsty ass hoe was working with.

JAE

I had been a sitting duck outside the hospital, waiting for nearly 20 minutes, for Trap to push Rocket out of the main door.

"A weh deh bumbaclath em a duh," I said, getting out the parked car at the entrance of the building. I was so irritated when wondering what the fuck they were doing that I left the motor running.

I got to the room in seconds. I heard Trap laughing his ass off so I thought they were just shooting the breeze, until I heard a bitch's voice.

"I wanna fuck with you."

Rocket told the bitch he was good, but she was determined to change his mind.

"Why, though?" she pressed.

"I've told you from day one that I was straight! Trap, let's go."

I smiled, knowing that Rocket had set that straight from the gate.

"Listen, I can be the side—"

I busted up in that bitch like the feds did at 2AM on a raid. Trap pulled his strap out, but when he saw my face he tucked that shit. Rocket seemed very calm, but the bitch looked like a deer caught in headlights. She ran behind

Rocket's wheelchair like I wasn't going to come after her. I went hard in the paint for whatever was mine; especially Rocket.

"Show that bitch ya' demo, Jae," Trap laughed.

"Nigga, you crazy!" Rocket barked angrily. "Grab Jae!"

When I heard Rocket tell Trap to grab me, I got real skillful like I was Steph Curry on the court, and spun around on that nigga, leaving his ankle swollen.

"Fuck!" Rocket shouted. He knew what time it was.

I had to get at least one punch in 'cause I had warned this hoe before.

"Get her!" the bitch screamed out.

I was determined for her to remember who the fuck I was. I leaped right over Rocket and clotheslined the bitch. Her eyes were the size of golf balls.

"What the fuck?" I heard Trap yelling.

I was raised on a farm so getting dirty wasn't nothing new to me.

"Arghhh!" She hollered after I threw that one punch that I wanted to.

"Get her up of off her, yo!" Rocket told bro.

Then, I felt hands pulling me up off the dumb bitch. I was swinging my feet like a windmill when I was coming up, praying one of my kicks would hit her in the face.

"Let me the fuck go, yo!" I screamed, but Trap's grip got tighter and tighter under my chest.

"Jae, that's enough," Rocket said, looking at me.

I knew I had to calm the fuck down. His voice spoke volumes. Thank God security wasn't all over the room with all the noise I had just made when knocking this bitch down.

Trap didn't put me down until I got my heartrate down. The bitch took a few minutes to get

up off the floor, holding her neck and back. I wanted to go the fuck off on Rocket, but I would never disrespect him in front of no bitch. So, I fixed my clothes and walked out the room, rolling my eyes. Before I died, I knew I was going to body me a bitch over that nigga.

***

"You can't keep fighting and you pregnant, sis." Chessan was preaching to me in the car while I was waiting for Trap and Rocket to come out of the building. I'd already gotten his discharge papers, so what the fuck was still taking him that long to come the fuck out?

"Yea, you right, but a bitch not gonna keep testing me like I'm a bitch!" And I meant that. I didn't give a fuck if I was having a baby, I was gonna continue to show my ass. My hands ain't ever failed me.

"Rocket is a handsome dude. Bitches gonna flock to him, but he loves you, Jae."

"I hear you. Here they come. I'll see you soon." I ended our conversation, keeping my face straight ahead.

Trap opened the passenger door. "You know that nigga loves you and only you!"

I pretended like I didn't hear him say that. He helped Rocket into the front seat before he closed the door. I looked in the side view mirror to see Trap folding up the wheelchair. He unlocked the back door and loaded the chair in before he walked behind the car and entered, sitting behind me. I pulled off, feeling Rocket's eyes on me.

"Speak ya' mind," he said.

I took a deep breath as I turned left at the light. "If a nigga kept coming at me, you would've smoked his ass before he completed the sentence."

"You know this, so what's your point?"

"My point is, you always saving a bitch from an ass beating."

"Trap is on the run; you forgot?"

I gripped the steering wheel with both hands. I was turning red in the face.

Rocket waved his finger from side to side. "I don't want none of them bitches out there! You the only one for me, so that shit them bitches do and say shouldn't matter."

"Really?" I chuckled.

"Jae, don't get fucked up," he said, like I was supposed to scared when I bodied mufuckas like he did. Truthfully, I was scared to body his ass.

"I'ma let you have that." I turned the system up. As long as I was with him, I was going to keep swinging on bitches like Tiger Woods' wife.

"But, Rocket, you can't say that shit wasn't funny," Trap laughed, breaking the tension in the car. "Jae be knocking them bitches down."

That brought a smile to my face. Rocket shook his head 'cause he knew when it came down to me throwing my hands, I was a beast.

"I'ma start toe tagging them bitches. I'm way too pretty to keep fighting."

CHAPTER 17
ROCKET

Gotti had Jae moved a few days before I got out. She was no longer in Crown Heights but she was still in Brooklyn, though.

"Run Crown Heights, but stay out of Crown Heights until you can actually run and jump again." Those words were my father's.

Pulling up in the suburban area had me feeling safe, but I knew better. When you had beef, nowhere was safe; not even hell. I knew Jae was in her feelings, but she knew my heart, soul and body was hers, and no one could change that.

Jae pushed a button on her phone, which made the gate in front of us rise. Once we were inside, she pressed the button once more, to have the gate fall behind us.

"You like it out here?" I asked her.

"It's alright. Better, now that you are here with me."

Our house had a wall on both sides. I figured it surrounded the crib. The ride was short from the gate. The garage door in front of us let up, where a black Suburban and a cream-colored Chevy Impala was hiding. Jae parked between them, then closed off the garage.

"Welcome home, bruh," Trap sounded off.

"It feels good already, my nigga."

"Bring him in, Trap!" Jae said like a Boss. I couldn't help but to smile. She got out the car and disappeared through a door on the left.

Trap helped me out the car and into the wheelchair. My body was sore, but I knew that with time and some exercise I would to be back in no time. Trap opened the same door that Jae had entered, and pushed my wheelchair through.

"Welcome home!" They screamed.

Jae was standing beside a nigga, and beside that nigga was a female and two more niggas. I could tell that they were all related from their smiles and facial structure.

"This is JJ, Chessan, TT and Chris. They're my siblings." Jae introduced me to her family. This wasn't my first time seeing them. I'd seen their pictures in her apartment that day she saved me when I was running from the police.

"What's good?"

Her sister, Chessan stepped forward and kissed me on my cheek. I watched Jae's face, and she showed no emotions. Her brothers moved to me one by one, shaking my hand. I could feel the love that they had for me right then. Trap dapped them all up, but fool kept his eyes on Chessan. He wasn't slick at all.

***

After a nice home cooked meal, my sister-in-law and Jae showed me around the lower part of the house.

"There's six bedrooms, four and a half bathrooms, and a full basement with a room for Trap. I know you always want ya' right hand close."

I looked at her when she was taking my flip-flops off my feet. She knew me better than I knew myself sometimes.

"The girls won't have to share a room when my family goes back."

"I don't know how I could ever repay you for all you've done for me," I said.

Jae walked away from me, toward a door. She opened it, showing me a full bathroom. My eyes didn't leave her when she bent over and turned the water on in the tub. I couldn't wait to tear that pussy up.

"You can promise to spend the rest of your life with me!" she exclaimed.

"You ain't said shit, baby."

She turned to me, broadcasting that smile I would die for. "I'm so happy that you are home." She then squatted in front of me.

I leaned forward, connecting our lips. "Me, too," I said once I was satisfied with the taste of her lips.

***

The Queen helped me use the bathroom, wiped my ass and took a bath with me. Every time she washed where I had been shot, she'd kiss the scars.

"Ayo, I love you, gorgeous; real spit!" I said, cupping her face in my hands. "Don't ever take it for granted, you hear me?"

I told her to stand up so I could admire her body. Her baby bulge was beautiful. Her body was like perfect artwork. I licked my lips and leaned my head back on the tub. "Come let me taste that."

When the pum pum touched my lips, my dick got rock hard, but I knew I couldn't put any pressure on my legs and work the pussy with my wood. My tongue had to do for the moment.

"Arghhhh!" She threw her head back in pleasure, holding on to the wall for support.

I spread her legs, getting my tongue all the way up in her ocean. Then, I nibbled on her clit for a second, only to swipe her pussy with my tongue.

"Rocket." She dipped her body before she stood back up on shaking legs.

I pushed my tongue deeper inside of her, commanding her body to release the juices that I longed for.

"Babi." She hit her fist against the tile three times as she blessed me with her coconut juice.

"I love you always," I said, before sucking her dry.

"I love you, too."

Jae wanted to blow me off, but I only wanted to make her explode. She washed me up, then herself, before she got me out and dried me off. I could move a little on my legs, so that helped her out a lot.

While she got dressed, I called Trap on my phone. "Gather Jae's brothers and meet me in the living room. Leave her sister alone, bruh."

"Aite." He laughed, ending the call.

JAE

I wheeled Rocket into the formal living area, then dipped to check on my sister. Chessan was laying across her bed in a pair of boy shorts and a tank top, talking on her phone.

"Mi can't mek er chat tu yuh, daddi," she said, acknowledging my presence with a smile. She was on the phone with our father, according to the conversation that she was having. She got quite for a second, and I figured that our father was talking. "Okay, mi a guh tell er and mi luv yuh, tu." She threw the phone on the bed as she rolled over to sit up.

I was looking out the window at the stars.

"Sis, I know you don't want to hear what I have to say, but please just listen."

It was a beautiful night, period. Rocket was finally home, where he belonged, I had a few of my siblings with me, and I was expecting a bundle of joy soon. “Go ahead, I’m listening.” I didn’t turn around.

“You need to talk to daddy. He loves you, no matter if you think he don’t—”

“How could he love me when he had the chance to show me, and he didn’t?” Tears moistened my eyes. Talking about my parents was a tremendously touchy subject.

“That’s why you need to talk to him, Jae.”

I turned around to face my best friend, my blood. Tears danced down my face. “I didn’t have either parent there to raise me, Chessan. At least you had ya’ mother. My grandparents loved me when they didn’t have to. It wasn’t their job; it was my parents’!”

She knew I was spitting some real live shit, so she didn’t comment.

“Look how many of us he had, and how many of us did he raise?” I didn’t wipe my tears away. I needed to get this shit out so it wouldn’t eat me alive anymore. Chessan had yet to answer the question, so I did for her. “None, sis. Not one. And he say he loves me?”

“Jae, he does! He just don’t know how to show you when you blocking him out.”

I shook my head, feeling depressed and mad as fuck ‘cause Rocket told me to let it go, but here I was opening up the casket again. “Blocking him out? Are you serious?”

“Yea, he get that he fucked up. Now that he’s older, he regrets not being there for all of us when we were growing up. I watched and listened to him one day under the mango tree at grandma’s house, praying to God to watch over all his kids.” Tears were now in her eyes. She was choked up as she walked toward me. “We share the same father; all eighteen of us. You are the only one that hasn’t forgiven him, Jae." She opened her arms, and I fell inside them, crying my eyes out.

I knew I had to the storm one day with my parents, but I just wasn't ready for that to happen. What would happen if they didn't say something that I wanted to hear?

"Shit don't turn sweet overnight. Just think about listening to him, please."

The more my sister begged me, the more I cried. My hormones had me fucked up, or maybe I just needed to get the shit off my chest and find out why my parents left me.

Chessan pulled away and stared into my eyes for an answer.

"I promise," I said.

Together, we wipe one another's tears away.

***

Once I left Chessan, I went to bed. Rocket was still hanging out with the fellows when I laid down. I thought about how my parents abandoned me, and they were alive. There was no way in hell I would just up and leave my child. The only way that would happen was if I was dead, Other than that, I was going to there to teach, protect and love them.

I rubbed my stomach as tears returned. This time, I let them run past my ears, staining my pillow. I had to get all this shit out. I needed my mind clear for when I hit the streets. A weak mind always left space for a fuck up, and I couldn't afford to fuck up. Rocket needed me to be on point and alert for us as a family.

I said my prayers, thanking the man above for his many blessing that he'd bestowed upon my life. No matter all the tribulations that I had encountered, I had made it out as a survivor.

***

I woke up with Rocket's hand on my stomach and my cell phone going the fuck off. I tried to get up without waking Rocket, but it didn't work. He looked at me as soon as I answered my call.

"Hello?"

"Sorry to wake you up so early," Gotti apologized.

I hit the speaker button to see that it was 5:30AM. "You good."

"I am good, but one of the projects got hit about an hour ago."

"Which one?" I asked, getting up to get dressed.

Rocket tried getting up, but I pushed him back down on the bed. I was waiting on Gatti to say JMoney's joint, but he didn't.

"Park Rock Rehab."

"What?"

The nigga Goon that ran that joint lived by his name, so I knew he showed the fuck out.

"But it's not the police that hit them."

"Huh?" I stopped dead in my tracks.

"It was a shootout."

"With who?"

"I'm not sure, but I'm on my way over there, now."

"Gotti, you can chill. I got this!"

"Jae, fuck that! You're pregnant! Sit yo' ass down and let me handle this. You're a boss. It's okay to play the background at times"

"Fuck the background, nigga. I'm a frontline bitch." I ended the call on his ass.

Yeah, I was bunned up and moving kind of reckless, considering my pregnancy. But when murder was in my eyes I had zero understanding.

Rocket tried to talk some sense into me, but his words didn't penetrate.

"Babi, stop worrying. I got this, man." I assured him.

Concluding that he couldn't stop me from going to do what I had to do, he insisted, "I'm coming with you!"

As he struggled to get up, I saw pain written all over his face.

"No, you not." I was already dressed in all black. "I'll be back!" I kissed his lips.

"Jae!" he called out when my hand touched the door knob.

Defiantly, I pushed on without turning to answer him.

I dashed up the stairs to Chessan's room, waking her up out of her sleep. "Sis, I gotta make a move, so I need you to help Rocket out till I'm back!"

"Huh?" She was still sleeping.

"Wake ya' ass up and help Rocket out. I'll be back."

"Okay." She was up and wiping sleep out of her eyes.

"And put some damn clothes on, too."

"I wouldn't want Rocket to leave you for me." The TV was on so I saw her smile.

"If he did, y'all wouldn't live to see another day." My comment came from the heart.

It removed the smile off her face and it was my time to laugh, but I was fucking serious. It wasn't nothing for me to whack that ass. Blood or not.

I woke Trap and my brothers up, telling them we had to bounce. "I'll be in the Suburban waiting."

Rocket's ringtone went off as I was waiting on them niggas to come on. "You strap?" He asked.

"I'm always dirty. I take a shit with it in my hand, fuck with it under my pillow, and sleep with it by the bed."

"Say no more. I love you."

"I love you, too."

Trap sat up front with me while my brothers filled the back up. I hit the alarm system on the house before I pulled out onto the street.

"What the fuck going on?" Trap asked.

"Gotti called me, saying how Goon's spot got hit, and it wasn't the boys in blue."

I heard guns loading and clocking in the back.

"Did he say who it was?"

"Naw, he don't know." I checked to make sure I was doing the speed limit as I moved around in the early morning traffic. The ride was silent.

When I arrived at the scene, flashing red and blue lights were everywhere, so I circled the block and parked a few blocks around the corner. As soon as my feet hit the pavement, I called Goon's phone.

"Boss, this shit is crazy," he said as soon as he picked up.

"I see."

"You out here?"

"I ride for mine. Where you at?"

The crew was walking with me. He told me he was out in the crowd that had gathered in front the building. All the police lights made it seem like it was broad day light, so it wasn't hard to spot him. Goon was about 5-feet-11 inches, 220 pounds, and light skin. He looked like he could be a football player, but he was a trapper. Even though his team was small, they were go-getters. They grew up together, eating peanut butter sandwiched and drinking Kool-Aid for dinner. They knew the struggle, so they appreciated the love Rocket showed them. He didn't charge them the same pricelike he did everyone else.

Police officers were out walking the streets, asking anyone if they had seen or heard anything, but all I heard was no. Mufuckas lived by that no snitching law ‘cause they knew that shit was way deeper than just telling. It meant death.

“Let’s walk.” I suggested.

“Aite.”

We circled the block while Goon explained what had happened to me. Trap and Chris stayed back to check shit out. JJ was leading the way with TT behind me and Goon.

“How many soldiers get murked?”

“Two, yo.” I heard sadness in his voice. “Them niggas were my brothers!” He punched his palm with his fist. He was hurting. Death had a way of breaking the strongest mufucka down to a baby, but you had to be a warrior to overcome that shit.

The story I got from Goon was that a van came through, trying to buy some heavy work, but when one of the niggas said they didn’t roll like that a dude started shooting, and two niggas lost their lives.

“So, where the paper at?” After the little shootout between Goon and the niggas, the shooters threw a piece of paper out the window before they sped away.

Goon pulled the white paper from his pocket, handing it to me. It didn’t take me long to figure out who the shooter was affiliated with. I read it over and over again before I stuffed it in my pocket.

“Who else know about the paper?” I stopped and so did everyone else.

“No one!”

“Keep it that way.”

CHAPTER 18
ROCKET

There was no way in hell I was going back to sleep after Jae bounced, so I got myself up and handled my hygiene. It was hard and painful, but I was determined to get back on my feet. I pushed through the pain. I wheeled myself into the kitchen to find Chessan standing around the stove, cooking.

"Good morning," she greeted me.

"What's up?"

Jae talked about their bond all the time to me. Shorty had her back when I was tackled, heavy. The more I looked at her, the more I noticed that she was beautiful. No wonder Trap couldn't keep his eyes off of her. Her hair was resting in the middle of her back, and her complexion was a shade darker than Jae's. She was young but her body displayed something different. Lil' Mama was bad, but she wasn't as gutta as my woman. Plus, she wasn't my type, and I damn sure didn't roll like that. They, were blood.

Snapping out of my trans, I wheeled into the living room to watch the news. Pictures of myself, Jae's family and herself, plus the girls were on the wall around the house, along with the Jamaican flag. The way she laced the crib let me know that I had finally made it where I wanted to be in the game.

Chessan brought me a healthy plate of three French toast, two boiled eggs and some grits with butter and orange juice as the beverage.

"Thank you," I said.

"You are welcome." She then turned the 62-inch flat screen on. "Anything yuh wanna watch?" This was my first time actually hearing a little bit of her Jamaican accent. She lived in the UK where they spoke proper English.

"Yea, the news, but I really wanna talk to you about something serious."

The look on her face let me know that she didn't expect that from me. She took a seat across from me with her face on the TV.

"I plan on asking ya' sister to marry me."

When she smiled at me, I swore I was staring at Jae. Damn.

"She loves you more than life itself." Her statement didn't surprise me. Jae's actions had shown me that. "I told her how crazy she was to put her life on hold for you, but she told me real love was hard to come by."

I dug into the food she'd made me while listening to her. Jae didn't keep anything away from her sister. Chessan knew everything. I pondered on if Jae had even told her sister how good the dick was.

"Congrats on the baby, too."

"Thank you."

The food was on point. It wasn't like Jae's, but it was good. She got up and removed the plate from my hand, handing me the remote in return.

"Thanks for breakfast."

"No problem. It's my job to take care of you when my sister is not here, or whenever she needs me to." She walked away, leaving me with a thought. *Are all Jamaican women this damn good to their men?*

Nothing was going on CNN so I changed the channel to music videos. It was mad funny to me how niggas rapped about the game and didn't know shit about it. Mufuckas sold millions off shit they didn't have a clue about.

Chessan returned after she'd cleaned the kitchen up. "How are you feeling?" She took her seat again.

"I'm good. Breathing." I kept my eyes on the TV.

"That's a blessing."

This was my second time getting hit up and I survived. They said a cat had nine lives, and I wondered if I'd ever be that lucky. It was almost 7AM so I switched the station to the local news to see what was going on in the borough, to take my mind off of death.

"You have a set date for the wedding?" she suddenly asked me.

"In a way, I do. It has to be private. The only people I want there is family, and I can count those people on both of my hands."

She bobbed her head.

"It must be a surprise. I don't want Jae to have a clue about this and—"

"Police are still investigating the brutal murder of Ricardo Johnson."

I turned the volume up, making sure I didn't miss anything that the anchor lady was saying.

"His body was found last week by his parents outside their home on their porch. The NYPD has offered five thousand dollars for any information about his death." They showed a picture of Ro in his early days with braids.

That's all Ro's life meant to the system. The system that he'd been loyal to.

"It's a very disturbing story, Shawn," the news lady expressed to her co-worker on set.

"Yes, it is. The burial service will be this Saturday at one in the afternoon, at the First Baptist Church, on President Street."

"Jae, told me how she made him suffer for what he did to you," Chessan chimed in.

"Breaking news." The screen flashed to the Park Rock Projects. "Early this morning, shots rang out, leaving two African American men dead," the reporter said. They broadcasted the building that Goon ran. "As you can see, police are still out here, trying to piece together any information that they can get. The local hotline number is below. If you can provide any information about this, please call your local police station. Back to you Shawn."

I reduced the volume. "Mufuckas gonna know not to fuck with my squad! If it's war mufuckas wants, its war they gonna get!"

JAE

Rocket was walking on his own at a slow pace when I entered the house. We all stood back and watched him move. He missed the streets, so I knew he would be very determined to get back on his toes so he could reunite with his true love. The streets. He was sweating something seriously, and I could only imagine how bad he was hurting. His steps were small, his hands were shaking as his legs wobbled under him, but he kept pushing. He was adamant to get well fast.

"How long you been at this?"

He stopped. I was at his side. Trap and my brothers had yet to move.

"For a while." His breathing was short and I knew he was tired, so I threw his arm over my shoulder and we walked to the sofa, together.

"Grandma raised you great, Jae," JJ said, pushing the wheelchair over to us.

Rocket replied for me. "She did, and it's a must that I meet and thank her."

***

I spoke to Rocket once the room cleared out, telling him the story that I got from Goon. "This shit is crazy, babi." I pulled the paper out of my pocket, handing it to him.

"Cubans, are better than Americans, bitch." Rocket finally read the words out loud. The shooting came from Cuba's team.

I was waiting on Rocket's voice to boom off the walls, but it never came. He stood up, and I was up too.

"I got it," he said.

I sat back down, watching him as he took a step. My heart ached because I knew he was in pain.

"Ro's service is Saturday, and we're going." He took another step as his voice clapped like thunder.

This day was Thursday.

"Okay." I got up off the sofa to get him some water to drink. When I got back, he had made his way across the room. I gave him the water bottle once I was near him.

"Thanks." He took the bottle without stopping. "Let Goon know that we are paying for the two trappers' funerals."

"Okay. And I had planned to be there, representing us as they are laid to rest."

Lines formed in his forehead, so I knew he was thinking, hard. "Who you taking with you?"

"Who you want me to take?"

"Trap!"

ROCKET

When Jae and her brothers left to go check on all the projects, Ms. Judith, my seeds and Chessan got to work.

Trap had got me exactly what I needed. All I was waiting on was Jae to show up.

"How you feeling?" Ms. Judith asked me while we were waiting.

"Good." I really was. I had pushed the streets to the back of my head for the day.

"She's back," MooMoo and MiMi yelled.

I took a deep breath, moving into my position. As soon as the door open, MooMoo pressed play on the stereo system.

"Who wants the perfect love story anyway, anyway? Cliche, cliche, cliche, cliche Who wants that hero love that saves the day, anyway?" Beyoncé sang.

Jae's face was stuck. The room was decorated in light blue and lavender. Balloons and roses were all over the place, along with a red carpet for her to walk on. Trap was my best man, and Chessan was her maid of honor. MiMi stepped from the side, throwing flowers on the carpet, making way to where I was.

"You just gonna stand there?" Jae asked. I was standing on my own. She smiled and looked back at her brothers.

I had gotten their blessings. Everyone knew about this except for her.

"Boy meets girl. Girl, perfect women. Girl get to bustin' before the cops come running. Uh. Chucking deuces, chugging D'usse—" Jay Z was spitting how I was feeling.

She glowed the whole walk to me with her family behind her. MooMoo decreased the music when Jae was standing beside me.

"This how you do?" Jae laughed, with her eyes on her clothes.

"We said our wedding day would be way different, remember?"

She nodded. She was still sexy in her jeans and Jay's. I had kept the shit simple, too. True's on my body and timbs on my feet. Gangstas did shit differently, anyway.

"You ready?"

"Babi, come on now, I was born ready."

We faced the pastor from Ms. Judith's church together.

"This is the day that the Lord has made. Let us rejoice and be glad in it." He read from the bible. "I'm here to join you two together as one under God."

Jae was all teeth. Chessan was crying already. Trap handed the rings to the pastor.

"Draymond Wallace, do you have anything to say to your soon to be bride?"

I turned to face Jae. "Since day one, you've kept it so real and raw. You held me down for them three years like it was nothing. I can't repay you, but I will die trying. I love who you are as a person. I love how you love my kids like they are yours. And thanks for making me a father, again."

"Ohhhhh," I heard Ms. Judith and the girls' voices.

Trap touched me on my shoulder.

"I just want you to know that I love you so much, Jae."

She mouthed back, "I love you, too."

"Jae, do you have anything you'd like to say?" the pastor asked.

She cleared her throat and smile. "You've been in my corner like a trainer from day one. I will never leave you. I'll be ya' shoulder whenever you need one. Nothing or no one will ever come between us." Everything she said, I knew it came from her heart. "You're my nigga, my thugga and I'm riding with you no matter what. I'm in this for the long haul. If you fall, I'm falling with you. If you ball, I'm balling with you. As long as we have each other, we'll be alright. I love you, Draymond."

Thugs do cry. I couldn't help the tears from falling down my face. I looked around the room to see that I wasn't the only one crying.

"As you put these stones on, repeat after me," the pastor prompted us.

The 2.3 carat Vera Wang Love Collection diamond ring that Trap had gotten was perfect for my Queen. As I placed the ring on her finger, I repeated what the pastor said. Tears were now streaming down Jae's face.

"I do!" My legs were killing me from standing so damn long, but I couldn't give up.

It was Jae's turn to put my ring on my finger. My shit was that, too. Altogether Trap had spent over thirty bands on our rings.

"I do!" she sang, looking at her bling.

"You may now kiss your bride," the pastor said.

When our lips touched, I tasted heaven on earth. Jae had been my star. When I was down and out, she was there riding with me on a flat tire. When my kids' mamas stepped out of line, she was there to put them back in line. She had shown me the true meaning of love in this game by busting her guns for me and with me. Loyalty was hard to come by, especially in a female, but she bled that shit.

"I now pronounce to you, Mr. and Mrs. Draymond Wallace."

Once we turned around to face the family, they all started clapping.

CHAPTER 19
JAE

I was officially muthafuckin' Mrs. Wallace, and not even death could take that from me. We were finally one— for better, for worse, till death do us part.

After the ceremony, we all sat down and enjoyed the evening, thanks to the catering that Ms. Judith had provided. She was so damn happy, it was written all over her face.

Trap was the first one to make a toast. "Rocket, bruh," he raised his glass. "Congrats. Out of all the females you've had, I must say no one go as hard as Jae." The room cracked up, even the girls. "Sometimes, I'm scared for you, 'cause she is a crazy Jamaican. But I know the love she do have for you is perfect."

"Awwww," Chessan squealed, batting her lashes at Trap.

"Jae, thanks for having my brother's back the way you do." I smiled and leaned my head towards Rocket. "I love the both of y'all and can't wait to meet the new member of the family."

"Thank you," I spoke up for me and Rocket.

When everyone was making their toasts, I realized just how happy they were for us.

"I'm praying that you'll have a boy," Ms. Judith beamed with love.

"A boy?" MiMi asked unhappily.

"We want another sister," MooMoo said with finality.

"As long as the baby is healthy, I don't care what you have." Chessan rubbed my stomach.

Hours passed. We talked the night away.

"I wish we could be here all night, but I have to get my pastor and these girls home," Ms. Judith said, getting up and gathering her things.

The girls didn't want to leave, but Rocket promised them that they would be here next weekend for good. As they said their goodbye's, me and Chessan started to clean up the place.

"Yuh ave if ave anada wedding, Jae."

"Wah mek yuh seh su?"

She suggested that I had to have another wedding and I wanted to know why.

"'Cause grandma and grandpa deserve to see you walking down the aisle, smiling." She stacked the dishes up in the sink. "And, have daddy walk you to your king."

I stopped sweeping when I heard her last statement. I knew she was right, but I continued to sweep, listening to Rocket, Trap and my brothers drinking and talking.

It took us about three hours to get the place back in order. I was hella tired and so was Chessan, even though I left her and Trap together in the living room talking. When our bedroom door closed, I headed straight for the shower.

Rocket climbed in the bed. I hadn't had time to soak up everything until now. As the hot water hit my body, I closed my eyes, playing back my sister's words. *"Just hear daddy out."*

Ro's farewell day was near, the goons that lost their lives had to be laid to rest, and Cuba had to be found. On top of that, other shit needed to be done.

The moment that I was floating in, however, was that I was married to Rocket. I soaped up and washed quickly so I could celebrate my wedding night the proper way, 'cause a honeymoon was out of the question for right now.

Rocket was awake, looking at the flat screen with his shirt off.

"I thought you'd be knocked out with all that drinking you'd been doing." Water was dripping off my body as I stood in front of the screen.

"Climb in the bed and put me to sleep, then."

Rude boy didn't have to say it but that one time, and I was on him like a tick on a dog.

Rocket had always been a freak with me, but tonight was my night to make that ass tap the fuck out with two fingers in his mouth.

I started with his toes in my mouth before I licked the bottom of his feet. His body was no longer just his, but it was also mine. He stared down at me as my tongue moved in and out from between his toes. I was his gangsta in the streets and his freak in the sheets.

"Damn!" He growled like a tiger.

For several long seconds, the only sound was the wet sucking noise. Then, I glided up to the bulge in his boxers. Slowly, I took his boxers off with my teeth. When his dick was free, I licked the head of it, watching it grow in front of me.

"I want you to ride me like you never have before." His fingers brushed my skin, lightly, causing my nipples to harden.

The burning ache between my legs caused my body to tremble.

"Ride me," he demanded.

I bit my lip but complied, squatting over him to welcome his dick. "If at any time you want me to stop 'cause I'm hurting you, let me know."

Rocket smiled, but he never answered.

When he filled me up, my body lurched forward. I rested my hands on his chest as I moved up and down. Rocket sat up, locking his lips around my nipples. The sensation that came over my body pushed me to ride him faster. His hands gripped my cheeks, spreading them further apart. With every thrust, the more I wanted, the more I craved for him to push up in me, harder. His finger found my pussy, and as soon as he touched my clit, my body exploded like a firecracker. My head leaned back as I cried out, feeling the explosion rock me. The more Rocket continued to pump in me and massage my clit, the more I bounced up and down, squeezing my muscles. As Rocket's body worked deep, an uncontrollable feeling came over my body. It started in my toes and worked its way up to my pussy. My muscles tightened, and all I could do was scream.

"Oh my God!"

He dropped his head in my neck, kissing and biting my skin. I closed my eyes against the sudden burst of pleasure that he had exploded in me. I clung to him with all my strength. This had been one of the best sexual experiences in my life.

His hips worked back and forth, like he hadn't got hit up weeks ago. He plunged deeper one last time before he collapsed backwards onto the bed with his eyes closed.

"That's all you got to give ya' wife on her wedding night?" I asked gruffly.

He wrapped his arms around my waist, and I felt his dick growing inside of me. "Naw, I'm just warming up, Mrs. Wallace."

My pussy twitched, just thinking of how he was about to handle me.

ROCKET

Jae had a nigga's toes curled the fuck up last night, but once I got back up in them guts, I had her ass begging. I made that pussy pay. She tapped out first. I closed my eyes for only a few hours, but that was it. After, I was wired up.

For Cuba to touch one of mine brought heat to my bones. I sweated, trapped and bled for that clown. Since I didn't want to contribute to his operation anymore, he wanted to show me his so-called power. One thing about me that he should've remembered was that I was always a rider for mine.

"Can't sleep?" asked Jae as she sat up beside me on the bed.

"I won't sleep good till that mufucka is dead."

"He's not the only one that we have to worry about." Jae put her hand on top of my leg.

My mom and that bitch ass nigga has got to pay, and they will. The greatest element of surprise is, death.

"I know. Get dressed." I was up and in a pair of boxers within seconds.

"Does it matter how I'm dressed?" She smirked.

"I don't care if you are naked. As long as you got my back."

"And that you know I do!"

***

The early bird got the most worms. Beam was out on the block with a few of his crew when I was rolling through. I pulled over to see what was up.

"What's good, son?" I dapped him up.

"You know I'm hungry, so I'm up eating"

Jae stepped out the car, checking out the surroundings. It was 5AM, but the way the fiends were coming back and forth, it looked like March Madness.

"How long you been out here?" I asked.

"Truth, called me around two this morning. Nigga ran through a whole fuckin' brick in four hours, my nigga!" There was pride in his voice.

"Word?"

"Hell yeah. So, I got dressed and showed up to provide for my crew. Can't have them niggas hungry."

Jae was standing behind me with her hand on her hip, looking amazing. I was blessed to have her.

"How shit going, otherwise?" I asked Beam.

"Shit is beautiful. Can't complain or lie. I've never seen the borough jump like this before."

A car pulled up down the street, just before the lights cut off. We all peeped game. Jae pulled her pistol out and kept it at her side. The streetlight allowed us to a little, but not enough to know who was in the car.

One of the block boys ran to the car with a bag in his hand, and within seconds the car left. Jae kept her strap out, though, until the car was out of sight. Beam looked at her and smiled, but her attention was still on the street.

"Be careful out here, son. The game is real," I spat to him. "Goon's spot got hit last night."

"That's what I heard." He stared at his team at work. "You have an idea who's responsible for it?"

Revenge ain't sweet if the news is out. "Naw."

"My ears is to the streets. As soon as I know something, I'll make sure you know."

What's understood doesn't need to be discussed. These niggas ride for me just like I ride for them.

***

"Hit the Brooklyn Bridge, baby."

Jae steered the car toward Fulton, as instructed.

"Give me ya' strap," I demanded.

She looked over to me and smiled. "Why would I do that when there's a heater under ya' seat?"

I sat up and reached under my seat to find exactly what she said was there.

"Locked and loaded!" That meant the clip was full.

"Thanks." I rubbed her thigh with my free hand, looking at the Brooklyn Bridge's lights ahead of us.

She changed lanes as I leaned my head back on the headrest with revenge at my fingertips. Jae turned the volume on the radio up, listening to a Reggae song.

"That's Garnet Silk, babi." She let her fingers dance on the steering wheel, as she sang along. "*Oh Jah, I'm depending on you.*"

Almost forty minutes later, I was where I wanted to be. "Take a left, park and cut the lights off."

Jae had done as she was told.

"Stay here. I'll be back."

"The only thing that will be staying here by itself is the car. I'm coming with you." Her tone was strong and demanding.

I shook my head, because her ass was so stubborn.

Jae pulled her left hand up, pointing at her wedding ring. "We're one!"

Finally, I gave in to her. "Leave the engine running."

She pulled her hair back inside a ponytail, then through her hood over her head.

People were up and heading for work. I waited until the cars passed before I opened my door. "Let's move."

We traveled a few houses up like a couple that was out for an early morning walk.

Jae constantly looked behind us. She had that predator gleam in her eyes and heart.

"Look to the left. White gate." I grabbed her hand as I spoke.

Her head moved in the direction for a split second. "Okay."

"Cuba's mother lives there."

"Oh yeah?" She pinched the inside of my hand. She's ready for whatever.

"Oh yeah."

CHAPTER 20
JAE

My sister and Trap were at the table when I got back home after our mission. It wasn't hard to tell that they were into each other, but she knew better. She was my sister, and he was considered my brother, which meant I didn't approve of them fucking around with each other.

"Weh aura broda dem deh?" I asked Chessan, mad as shit.

Trap raised his hands at my eyeroll. He was far from innocent. I didn't want my sister in our lifestyle. If I had the say-so, she wouldn't be.

"They're in the house, somewhere," Chessan answered me calmly.

"Let them talk," Rocket said, pulling me in the direction of our room.

"Thank you, brother-in-law!" Chessan shouted out excitedly.

When the door closed, Rocket got all in my ass for my attitude. "What was that about?"

"I don't want Chessan nowhere around this life!" I tucked my 9 under my pillow.

"You can't be serious."

"Yea! I'm dead ass fucking serious."

The stare he gave me told me to pipe it all the way down. I took a deep breath. He kicked his shoes off without a care in the world.

"She is my baby sister, babi."

"So?"

"I don't want her to be anything like me, Rocket."

"Do you even hear how you sound right now, Jae?"

He was right. We had the same blood pumping through our veins.

There was a tap at the door before I could continue.

"Who is it?" I called out.

"Chessan."

"Come in."

She had a look of embarrassment on her face, and I knew that she was pissed the fuck off. "Rocket, can you excuse us, please?" She requested.

He sliped inside his Jordan slides and exited the room.

"What's ya' problem?" She got right to the point instead of beating around the bush.

"I don't want you around Trap." With that, I sat on the edge of the bed with my eyes on hers.

"Why? Explain that to me."

I couldn't tell her that it was because of the lifestyle, because I'd look like a hypocrite.

"Huh?"

"This is not the life for you, Chess." I called her by the nickname that I gave her when she was a baby.

"I don't want to do all that crazy shit that you do." She sat beside me, then, with a softer voice. "He's a nice guy. He's here, I'm in the UK."

I looked at her sideways. "What that mean?"

"It means nothing, silly." She giggled. "He's got a situation, and so do I back in the UK."

"I hear you." It still didn't mean shit.

She hugged me. "I love you, overprotective sister."

"I love you, too."

"Anyway, I've got to get back to my job. Since Rocket is up and moving, I booked my plane ticket for Sunday."

"Good. You can come with me to lil' bro's going away party, then."

"When?"

"Today at one."

"Really?"

"Yup!"

She got up off of the bed, laughing. "You think you so smart."

"That I am."

I wasn't going to leave her around Trap by herself anymore. Well, I wasn't going to try.

***

As I chopped it up with my brothers, Chessan had her phone glued to her ear in a heated conversation. I made a mental note to ask her who she was talking to and what the problem was. I was already dressed and waiting. At the last minute, Rocket had invited Trap on the trip with us. Here I was, trying to keep Chessan away from Trap, only for Rocket to fuck it all up.

"Jae?" Rocket screamed for me.

"I'm in the living room, waiting on y'all!" I shouted back, causing Chess to cover up the mouth piece of her phone.

When Rocket and Trap set foot in the room, Chessan ended her phone call. Rocket was so damn sexy that my breath got caught in my chest. He had on a white button up Polo shirt, dark blue jeans, fresh out the box, all white high-top Air Force Ones, and a white and black New York Yankees fitted hat on his head. His white and gold diamond Rolex watch complimented his wedding ring on the same hand.

"You ready, baby?"

I licked my lips. My mind was no longer on this trip. I wanted him to clear the room out, bend me over the sofa and fuck my brains out.

"Babe?"

"Huh?" I shook my head. "What did you say?"

"I asked if you were ready."

"Yea, I'm ready."

"Let's bounce, then!"

***

The ride to President Street was a very silent one. I kept my eyes on Chessan and Trap the whole time. Neither one of them said a word to each other.

"Where am I supposed to park?" I asked Rocket as we pulled up at the church.

"It don't matter. Just park."

I found a parking spot, all the way in the back of the church's parking lot. We were already an hour late.

Rocket exited the Impala first, then walked around to open mine and my sister's door.

"Thank you," Chessan spoke, fixing her dress. For her to be attending a funeral, she was damn sure killing the show. Her hair was pinned up. The cream dress draped over her shoulders, cuffing her hips and her ass without fault. She had a body like a stallion. She wore my six-inch, black Red Bottoms like they were hers.

I kept my outfit effortless, even though I was matching Rocket. My hair was combed down from a wrap, and dark black shades hid my eyes.

Rocket reached his hand out and I grabbed it. My man had come a very long way.

He didn't limp for nothing. No one would've thought that months ago he had got wet up.

"Relax," I heard Trap telling Chessan.

"I'm trying."

Rocket clutched my hand tighter as we entered the church. The place was packed. It really amazed me how many people came out to salute a snitch.

"This shit is crazy," I mumbled, shaking my fucking head.

"In that we say, Amen." The pastor concluded his prayer.

"Amen." The congregation repeated.

I looked around the room, trying to see if I knew anyone, but I didn't. As Rocket stepped, I stepped. People in their seats stared at us as we moved up the aisle. My eyes locked in on Ro's bitch parents in the front row, but Rocket didn't stop until we were at the casket.

People started snickering and talking among themselves. Rocket released my hand and I turned around to mean mugged Rocket's mother the most. If looks could kill, that bitch would've been dead beside her bitch ass son, along with her disloyal, pussy cloth husband.

ROCKET

I knew Jae and Trap told me what had happened to Ro, but I had to make sure that the mufucka was dead for myself.

"No!" I heard my mother's cry as I touched the handle of the casket.

"Bitch, shut the fuck up, and stay seated!" Jae said brusquely, and the church got quiet.

The preacher didn't know what to say or do, so he just stood there, as stiff as a dead body.

I lifted the handle up, and the smell of death hit my nose, but I brushed that shit of by moving my nose upward. I had faced death before, and not once had it moved me.

The higher I hoisted the wooden handle up in the air, the stronger the odor got.

"Bitch ass nigga!" I let the handle go, seeing Ro's fucked up face.

The congregation started hollering. It wasn't a closed casket service anymore.

"You muthufucka—"

I spun around to find Jae ready to exercise her hands on Ro's pussy ass father. He had stood to his feet. This was the same bitch made nigga that got my father hammered by the system. The one that treated me like shit when I was a child. The mufucka that had something to do with me getting shot, too.

My mother bear-hugged his arm, trying to pull him back into the seat, but he pulled away from her. Hurt and pain was written all over their faces. Lack of sleep was evident under their eyes.

I extended my left hand out to Jae and she grabbed it. I didn't need a testimony against us, saying that we had threatened these mufuckin' bitch ass people. They knew what time it was and that's all that mattered.

A few steps down the walkway, I recognized a face that I wanted to see in the crowd. Not only was Cuba looking at me, he had Yellow Man's brother, Mayo, standing with him. They were mean mugging me. Jae released her hand from mine and I knew rude gal was ready to bust that joint in this bitch. Her DNA was one ofa fucking kind.

Trap and Chessan stood up from the last row. My nigga had spotted these clowns, too. He bopped his head in their direction, and I shook mine. There was a time and a place for everything. This wasn't the place or the time to pop off.

***

Jae sped out the parking lot with her .9mm on her right leg. I opened the glove box and remove the chrome 45.

"We going to the gravesite!" Jae said, hitting the brakes around the corner from the church. Her hair was pulled all the way back into a tight ponytail, already.

"Already," Trap agreed with her from the backseat.

"What you gotta say?" Jae asked me, sounding pissed the fuck off.

"You said it already." We were going to the gravesite.

***

We camped out around the block until the hearse passed us. The car windows were tinted as dark as night, so I wasn't worried about anyone spotting us. Jae maneuvered into the flow of traffic behind those who were going to pay their final respects to a snitch-born nigga.

The ride wasn't long or far from the church. Jae parked the car on the curb with the other motorists. I spotted a police cruiser in the cemetery, and since I was on probation, I locked the .45 back in the glove compartment, 'cause I knew Jae wouldn't depart from her 9.

"Bruh, you see that shit?" I asked Trap in reference to the police on duty.

"Yeah, I caught sight of that shit before Jae parked."

My eyeballs circled the place, looking for Cuba or Mayo, or anyone out of place, but I ended up with just Ro's parents and people I didn't know. Jae checked her phone quickly before putting it inside the middle console. Trap was already on the run for murdering that bitch ass nigga's family that took our brother, Tray, from us. And I damn sure wasn't going to put him in the hands of the law.

"Bruh, stay here with Chessan."

"What, nigga?" He answered like he hadn't heard me.

I turned around in the seat to face my brother from love, trust and loyalty. "Niggas ain't 'bout that life when them boys is present, so just chill."

He knew I made a lot of sense, but our bond had taught us better. When one moves, the other followed. He stared at me before he looked over at Jae, who was glaring at me.

"Jae, I ain't gotta tell you, but you already know. If you gotta fuck that trigger, fuck that bitch right!"

Jae's sister was just among us, shaking her head.

"Have I ever not fucked this bitch, right?" She raised the gun up off of her leg.

Trap and I knew the answer like we knew out ABC's.

"So, you already know I'ma fuck this bitch without grease!"

Chessan's jaw dropped when her sister spoke.

Jae tucked her pistol under her shirt before she exited the car with her ponytail bouncing from side to side.

"I married a mufuckin' Shotta fa real, son."

Chessan exploded with laughter as I made my departure.

JAE

The temperature out was just how I liked it. It was hot and humid. Fitting weather for my temper. We took a spot in the back, but not far away from the coffin. Rocket's mother was putting on a show for the people for real. I would've given the bitch the Greatest Mom Award if I didn't know her gave that bitch her opaque ass, first hand.

The bitch was hollering, "Why Jesus! Why my child!"

Her husband looked at her like the fraud she was. A lady was trying to hold her up but the bitch kept flopping down like a fish without water.

After taking my eyes off the performance of a lifetime, I noticed the police cruiser had two occupants.

Rocket whispered in my ear, telling me to look in a certain direction. My hand unconsciously touched my hip which I had done so. Cuba and Mayo had met up with us again. My man jerked my body in front of his, and I knew he was wishing that he'd brought his hammer with him. Simultaneously, he knew he was safe with me.

"Ashes to ashes, dust to—"

Raaaaatatttaaaaaa! The sound of distant gunfire erupted, cutting off the minister's words.

Rocket tackled me to the ground with his body on top of mine, pulling the handgun free from my waist. People were screaming and running as the semiautomatic flowed. It continued for seconds that seemed like forever.

I heard Rocket clicking the trigger, but nothing came out. "What the fuck?" He hollered in my ear. His body was blocking my view, so I couldn't see shit.

The fire continued and I knew whoever was squeezing the firearm was on a journey to wipe anything off this earth.

I pushed Rocket's arm from over my face so I could breathe and see. I saw a person hanging out a vehicle with a machine in their hands, spitting nothing but heat.

Skirrtttt! The car tires sounded, off lifting the dirt of the ground as it bolted away from the graceyard. Seconds passed before we moved.

"Oh my God!" People screamed. They were lucky to be alive, staggering to their feet.

Rocket eased his body up off me with a crazy look in his eyes. He pulled me up once he was on his feet. "What the fuck?" he asked, showing me the gun.

I hunched my shoulders as he tucked it in his waist. Then, I glanced over at the police cruiser to see the two white male officers laying on the ground, defeated. Bullet vests didn't protect

the head at all. Other bodies were riddled with heavy lead. Blood covered the green grass more than it would've been in a slaughter house.

I looked around for Cuba and Mayo while people were racing towards their cars, but them niggas never came into view. I also caught Ro's father getting up off of the ground, dusting his clothes off that were covered with bloody flesh. Astonishment was all over his face. Nowhere was safe for him. Not even the place where they laid the dead.

"No!" Ro's father screamed from the depth of his soul as he ran over to a body on the ground. "No! No!" He dropped to his knees and rolled the body over into his arms. The pain in his voice almost made me feel sorry for him. "No! No! No!"

Rocket looked at me and I smiled. His mother had gotten exactly what she deserved, just like I told him a while ago during a visitation when he was doing his bid. Karma was an ugly bitch.

Mr. Johnson clunge to his wife's lifeless body with tears exploding from his eyes. Some things are meant to be, and it was destined for that bitch to go out like that.

Rocket took a large amount of steps ahead of me en route to the coffin, which had sun beaming inside of it, thanks to the bullet holes. He freed his dick from his jeans and pissed all over the coffin as Mr. Johnson cried out to a dead body.

CHAPTER 21
ROCKET

Trap was in the front seat with the engine purring when we got back to the car. Chessan was laying across the backseat, reciting Psalms 23.

"Girl, I told you this ain't the life for you," Jae sang as she closed the door.

Trap pushed the pedal to the floor, getting us out of dodge. The sound of sirens filled the air as first responders of all kinds passed us.

"Slow down, my nigga," I prompted him. We had gotten away far enough without getting stopped when I got a glimpse of the black Buick that was in the cemetery letting lose. "That's the muthafuckin' car right there, yo!"

"Huh?" Jae responded, so I pointed to my left.

I snatched the pistol from my waist. It made Trap pull his too.

"No need to shoot," Jae said in a calm voice that caused me to look back at her. "It's Chris, TT and JJ."

Chessan looked over at her before she glanced at me, waiting for my response.

"What?" I focused my eyes back on the Buick.

The windows were dark tinted, so I couldn't see shit inside. When JJ showed his face outside the back window, I relaxed and I knew shit was real. Jae reached up front and got her phone out of the arm rest console as the Buick sped away.

I checked the pistol to see why the it wouldn't bark when I needed it to, finding that the clip was empty. The shit pissed me off. Jae knew better than that. What would've happened if her brothers didn't show up?

"Guh ova deh and mi a guh come get unno."

I turned around to see her on her phone. Her sister just kept shaking her head as if she had Parkinson's disease. Chessan was in dismay at what had happened.

I sat back and reflected on what had just happened to my mother while Trap drove. I didn't know my grandparents, but I wondered if her parents had loved her or hated her like how she despised me. It was fucked up that she was there when I got hit up, but it wasn't surprising to me at all. Me and Ro had bad blood. All she had to do was sit the fuck back and let us handle our beef, but she didn't. Instead, she took his side, like always. Now, she was laying right beside his snitching ass.

***

Jae asked for her gun when we got to the house. She was out the car and inside the crib before Trap had time to put the car in park. I was on her ass like air.

"The whole damn time, that shit was without bullets?" I was steaming mad because what would've happened if Cuba and Mayo had started shooting?

She was sitting on the bed with a pair of latex gloves that she got from out the dresser beside our bed.

"And when was you going to tell me that you gave ya' brothers the green light to do that shit?" I hit her with question after question while she loaded up the clip with some lead.

She looked up at me for a second, not saying a word as she kept inserting bullets into the clip. No matter how mad I was, seeing her filling the clip up moved my lips upward. She knew how to clean, load and unload a muthafuckin' pistol like a Seal Team Number Six member, and her shooting skills were of that, too.

"I know you mad right now," she eventually spoke, cocking a bullet into the chamber.

Mad wasn't a good word to describe me. I was infuriated. Here she was pregnant with my child and playing with fire without a bucket of water. Her normally calm demeanor was still on display.

"First of all, you would've been the first suspect to the police if ya' mom's dead body had been found elsewhere." She stood up and inserted the pistol in her jeans, behind her back. "So, when I ran the situation down to my siblings, they were down to complete it for me. And you and I know damn well that you don't kill females." She was staring me dead in my eyes. "I told them, to make sure that her husband didn't get touched, because I knew you wanted to dismantle that nigga ya' self." Her tone was still calm, cool and collected.

"I didn't tell you because I knew you would've disagreed. People saw us out there, and they knew had nothing to do with the shooting."

She had this shit planned all the way down to the T. My temperature dropped just a little as she explained her actions to me.

"It fucked me up when I saw Cuba and Mayo, but you've always told me, never let the enemy see you sweat." She was right. I did groom her right. "I touched my hip in the church to let them clowns know that I was packing and wasn't scared to test the sanctuary of a church out as my shooting range."

The temper I had when I first entered the room was now gone.

"And what would've happened if they would've gotten brave and started shooting?" I placed my hands on her shoulders.

"I would've jumped in front the bullets to make sure you didn't get hit!"

"Fuck is you saying yo? You carrying our seed! You can't be sacrificing the baby's life for mine. And, I don't want you to sacrifice your life for mine. Not like that! What kind of man do you think I am?"

Jae looked up at me with teary eyes. I could tell me reproach strung hard.

"Am I wrong for loving you more than I love anyone and anything?" she cried.

I pulled her into my arms as a glint of a tear formed inmy own eye. "I'm supposed to protect you with my life. I'd be less than a man to let you take a bullet for me," I preached, embracing her body tighter. Still, I knew everything that I was saying was just going through one ear and out the other.

"I love you, Rocket."

I never knew I could find love like this from a female. "I love you, too, Mrs. Wallace."

She pulled back, tipped on her toes and honored me with her lips. "I gotta go get my brothers." She pecked my lips one last time.

"I'ma ride with you."

JAE

I instructed my brothers to head to the Lynching Spot without stopping. When I texted JJ's phone, my crazy ass little bruh answered, *"A weh yuh deh?"* He was wanting to know where the hell I was.

"I'm on my way!" I texted back as I raced to them.

Rocket pulled his phone out and pressed a few buttons before setting it to his ear. "What's good with you, yo?"

I couldn't hear shit the person on the other end was saying, so I concentrated on the responsibility at hand. Traffic.

"My people's around ya' way. I need you to handle something for me."

I looked over at Rocket for a second, tantalized by his exotic eyes and his bossy voice.

"Bet!" He disconnected the call, resting the phone in his lap.

"Who was that?" I questioned him with my attention on the road, ahead and behind me, making sure I didn't have any unwanted visitors tailing me.

"JMoney." I could feel his eyes on me.

"What did he say?"

"He ain't said shit! That nigga better do as he's been told." Rocket's voice clapped like a rumble of thunder.

"You remember me telling you about Beam's remark?" Beam had let me know that he had heard what I did at the Lynching Spot, and I knew right then that JMoney had ran his fucking gums.

"Yea."

I turned on the street where the Lynching Spot was, seeing the black Buick with my brothers standing outside the car. There was only one building on this dead-end street and it was the building that I came face to face with Rocket in.

"And that shit is not acceptable." I spotted my target less than ten feet away from my folks. JMoney.

"You right," Rocket agreed.

"I'ma let that nigga breathe for right now." I parked the truck and jumped out before Rocket could respond. "Wah a gwan?" I greeted JJ with a thank you kiss on his cheek for the beautiful show he broadcasted earlier. "Where the hammers at?"

"Inna deh back pan deh seat."

I opened the back door and picked the guns up off of the backseat, feeling the heat still coming off them bad boys.

"Jae, ya' people's still run the auto body joint on Lefferts?" Rocket asked as he was dapping JMoney up.

I had run into this girl one day at the grocery store, and we exchanged numbers. Come to find out, she was the owner of the auto body shop, used as a trashing spot.

JMoney's eyes zoomed in on Rocket. It had been a hot minute since he'd last seen him in the flesh.

"Yea." My answer was unequivocal.

"Drive this joint over there so we can get rid of it, ASAP."

JMoney's face squished. "Right now?"

I looked at Rocket like, *I told you that nigga be questioning orders.*

"Yea, right now!" I barked before my man had time to. "I'ma bring you back to ya' whip."

"Aite." He locked white on white BMW, and followed me.

***

I navigated the Suburban with my family inside as JMoney followed. The stench from the backseat reminded me of Jamaica when the whiff of ganja hit my nostrils. I would've complained about the smoke, but after what my brothers had done, I figured they needed to smoke. Blowing down some weed is life for them.

"Fam." TT touched Rocket on his houlder. "Yuh wanna it dis?"

Rocket peeped over at me, but I didn't say anything. JJ and Chris laughed. They must've seen Rocket's face like I did. He reached back and took a hold of the lit blunt.

I kept my eyes on the road and JMoney. Rocket took a puff and almost coughed his lungs up.

I stretched out my right hand and patted his back, laughing my ass off. "Yuh gud?" I asked still laughing. My brothers had joined in, too.

He handed the blunt back, not attempting to take another puff. "What the fuck is that?" he questioned after he'd got himself under control.

"My youth, dat deh a gath!" One of my brothers responded.

Rocket turned around, facing my peeps with water running from his eyes. That's how bad he was coughing.

"Yea, mon," JJ answered, still cracking the fuck up.

I turned right, and JMoney did the same. We were at the destination, finally.

"Have the choppas out. I got to talk to old girl," I said, parking the truck. I motioned with my finger to JMoney, silently telling him to hold on.

He responded with a nod.

I headed inside and stopped at the front desk to speak to the receptionist. "Good day! Is Ribbon here?"

"Yes, she is." The receptionist let me know. "Take a seat while I give her a ring."

"Let her know it's Jae," I said before I went into the waiting room.

"I sure will."

Ribbon had the shop dazzled the fuck out with the simple arrangements that she had going on. A picture of the great Bab Marley with a spliff hanging out his mouth was painted above the vending machine. Mary Jane buds were pictured around the four walls. She was a Jamaican at heart, just like me, and she repped our country well.

A few ladies and an older gentleman were seated in the waiting room, reading magazines and watching CNN. I didn't take a seat. I looked out the door at the parking lot. Rocket and the crew, along with JMoney, were standing outside talking.

"Some baddi." Her accent was worse than mine. "Did someone requested to see me?" She switched to proper English. When I turned around and she saw my face, she squealed, "Jae!"

Even though we didn't hang out everyday or every month, we knew the bond that we had created that day in the grocery store was still there. Plus, we as Jamaicans stuck together like crabs in a bucket.

"Wah a gwan?" I beamed with joy as I approached to her.

"Long time nuh sey!" She opened up her arms. It had been a long time with us not seeing each other.

I recalled the day we crossed paths.

"Your total is one hundred and forty-two dollars and sixty cents." The clerk at the counter said.

Ribbon had all her grocery packed by the bagger as she dug into her purse for her money. "Damn!" She yelled in frustration as she came up with nothing.

The clerk was running out of patience as she blew bubbles from her gum.

Ribbon reached in her pants pocket, but she didn't come with a dime. "I'm sorry, I left my purse with my money at home," she said sounding and looking embarrassed.

The bagger started to unpack all the groceries into a shopping cart at the side.

"Here you go," I said, reaching up and leaning over my cart to pay the bubble popper.

The clerk looked at me like I had ten heads, but I was taught to bless people at any time, and my time had come to do just that.

"Yuh don't ave tu."

When I heard her Jamaican accent, it made me smile. Not only had I helped a sister out, but she was my people.

"Nuh sey su." I didn't want her to say that. She smiled and the rest was history.

We chopped it up in the parking lot that night like we had grown up together.

"How are the babies?" I asked. She had two little girls that she was raising by herself because their father was gunned down by some niggas that he was running with.

Thank goodness that he was smart enough to open up a body-slash- chop shop when he was in the game.

"Follow mi." She led the way to her office. "They are good," she said as I closed the door to her office.

We talked for about ten minutes before I got to why I was there.

"That's all yuh want?"

"Yea," I responded.

"Dat a nuh nuttin', rude gal!"

CHAPTER 22
ROCKET

"Dayummrnnnn a oow dat?" Jae's oldest brother, TT, gestured towards the girl that Jae was walking with. Once they were close enough, this fool TT walked up and kissed the woman's hand as he introduced himself.

"My youhh, really?" Jae looked at him and rolled her eyes.

"Yes, sis, really."

The sound of laughter filled our space in the parking lot as I watched Jae's and TT's interactions. TT had yet to release the lady's hand.

"Mi ive tings fi duh, yuh can cum bac lata." Jae said that shit so fucking fast that I didn't understand shit that she said.

"I'm going to get ya' number from my hating sister." TT released her hand.

I had to do a double-take because all of a sudden he could speak proper English.

"And you know ain't no hating in my blood, bruh." Jae paused and looked at the Buick. "I just wanna handle this shit real quick." She faced her brother with a serious look.

"Wha mek yuh tink seh mi a guh ge yuh fi mi numba?" The female spoke, staring TT the fuck down, but I saw through her look. If we weren't around, she'd probably give the nigga her draws.

"Yardie?" TT examined her, picking up on her accent.

I caught JMoney's eyes lingering over her body. Her micro braids were pulled up in a bun, showing off the gold necklace that circled her neck. She had yet to smile, so I didn't know what her grill looked like, but her jeans locked up her thighs and curves that were screaming from within.

To say she was thick was an understatement. She was thicker than a muthafuckin' frozen Sincker. The gray pullover she wore, stopped above her Gucci belt. She had money.

"Get the car through the gate." She turned around and pointed to a gate behind her, ignoring TT's question.

No matter how hard I tried not to look at her ass, I just couldn't help it.

"Gotdamn!" Someone yelled for me. Her shit was fat!

Jae turned back around and caught me looking at her people's ass. "Come on Ribbon," Jae said, walking off towards the gate. "Before I fuck around and act stupid."

I could hear Ribbon giggling as she walked away. I'm a nigga, but I'm not stupid. I'll look all day but I'll never dare step out on Jae and fuck our marriage up over some ass. Fuck no.

"Yo!" I shouted to JMoney, forcing his eyes off Ribbon's ass and over to me. "Drive that joint through the gate."

TT was still standing there watching old girl's hips rock from side to side. I couldn't help but to know what he was thinking.

JMoney cruised through the gate that Ribbon had instructed. It was a whole different place from the parking lot. There were thousands of cars— some damaged to the point of no repair, and some that needed to be worked on.

TT, Chris and JJ stayed behind.

Jae waved her hand at JMoeny for him to drive where she was pointing. There was a heavy-duty crusher in that direction. "Drive the car up on the metal ramp!" Jae yelled, but JMoney didn't hear her until he let the window down and she repeated herself.

He pulled up on the ramp under the metal plate above it and parked.

I stood back and watched as Jae and Ribbon walked up on the car. JMoney had cut the motor off and was about to exite the car but—

Blocka. Blocka. Blocka.

The bullets ripped his face open. The element of surprise was damn sure death. Ribbon didn't even flinch when Jae pulled the trigger, or when JMoney's face came flying off.

Blocka. Blocka.

The nigga's body jerked from the hot slugs. Jae tuck the pistol back in her jeans like nothing. Ribbon stepped down and around the car to the controller of the machine. Jae moved out the way and watched as Ribbon crushed the car and the body. By the time Ribbon was done handling the problem, the outcome was like a crushed sardine can.

I walked up behind Jae and wrapped my hands around her waist as I rubbed my unborn child. She didn't push me off, so I knew she wasn't that mad at me for staring at her people's ass.

"What I owe you?" Jae asked Ribbon, still in my embrace.

"Nothing you can't afford."

"Say the number." Jae dared her.

"What if I say, I want the people dead that killed Rich?"

"Ya' baby daddy?" Jae questioned.

"Yea."

"Give me the names and places and I'll be there!"

"That's it?" Ribbon seemed shocked by Jae's come back.

"That's it!"

"Say no more." I saw tears in Ribbon's eyes, and I could tell that she had wanted the muthafuckas dead that was responsible for her nigga's death.

I let Jae go so she could hug her people, and she did. I gave them some time and some space so they could vibe. Jae's brothers were higher than Whitney Houston and Bobby Brown put together when I got back to the truck.

"Where Jae?" one of them asked.

"She coming."

Jae ran to the truck, grabbed the guns and ran back to the back.

I knew she was going to kill JMoney, I just didn't know she was going to do it today. That nigga ran his mouth like a muthafuckin' bell about the wrong damn thing. A dead man can't be a witness to anything. Now, I had to find someone to run his spot.

"Where that nigga at?" JJ quizzed his sister as she shut the door.

"Sometimes a mufucka take ya' kindness for weakness, so sometimes you gotta blow their mufuckin' face off!"

I had married a monster.

JAE

JMoney had that shit knocking at his door, the day I found out that he had said something to Beam. I knew for a fact that he wouldn't have said shit else.

Ribbon had given me her number to give to my brother. "As soon as you find out who did that fuck boy shit, call me.

She had my back with the Buick and the body, so I had to repay her by eliminating them cowards that took her love away, for sure. She scratched my back, I scratch hers.

Chessan was leaving for the UK and my brothers were going back to Jamaica. We were all at LaGuardia Airport, waiting for the time to come so I could say goodbye. My brothers' plane was the first one to depart, so me and Chessan hugged them one last time before they entered the gate.

"Yo, if you need us, call us," JJ let me know, right in front of Rocket and Trap.

"You already know." I wanted to cry but I couldn't.

"Take care of my sister, yo." TT said to Rocket, dapping him up.

"You ain't said nothing, son." Rocket smirked.

"Bet!"

"Trap, my nigga, you family, yo," Chris told him, fist bumping Trap. These niggas were stuck in the house with Trap for weeks, so their bond had gotten that tight.

"Already." Trap responded.

I hugged Chessan as we watched them head through the tunnel and out of our sight.

"How you feeling?" Chessan asked me as we traveled away from TSA until it was time to board her plane.

"Sad but happy. I got to spend some time with ya'll."

"I know." Finally, she let me go. "Make sure you call daddy, too."

"I will."

"If I've got to come back over here just for you two, I will."

That made me laugh because I knew she would. She was determined to get us talking.

"I love you!"

"I love ya'll, too." She tapped my stomach.

"Trap!" she called.

I moved back so he could come forth.

When they hugged, I swear I felt like an intruder invading their space. Their connection was that strong that I could see it within their body language. What they had created in the little time was inevitable to happen. It was something I couldn't prevent if I wanted to.

"Ya' sister might be in love," Rocket whispered in my ear.

"Whatever," I mumble. "Ya' boy might be in love, instead."

Chessan pulled back and kissed Trap on his lips. I swear I saw sparks fly.

"I told you," Rocket had the nerve to say.

Damn, my sister had fallen for a thugga like I did. *Fuck!*

"Rocket, continue to love her like you love yourself. I love you, sis," she said, walking away from Trap.

This was my first time seeing Trap stuck and speechless. Nigga was in a trance.

"Let me find out!" I yelled loud enough for her to hear me around the noise in the airport.

She stopped and turned around. "You can't be the only one with a real gangsta in ya' life."

I looked at Trap as he watched Chessan step up to present her ID to an agent. If they took it seriously, I swear on my life, Trap better love her like Rocket loved me, or Rocket would be right handless, fucking with my sister's heart.

ROCKET

"Ma, you can go ahead and pack the girls up. I'm on my way to get them."

"Alright, I love you," she replied over the phone.

Jae was staring out the window when I got off the phone with Ms. Judith. She hadn't said a word since we left the airport, and I could tell that something was bothering her because her leg hadn't stop shaking.

"You good?" I placed my free hand on her moving leg.

"Yea, I'm gonna be okay." She stopped.

Something was under her skin and I needed her to let me know what it was so, I could help her erase the feeling that was hounding her. I kept my hand on her leg as I drove, letting her know that I was there for her.

Trap was on his phone. I couldn't read his mind 'cause that nigga never wore his feelings on his face.

"Yo, you good back there, my nigga?" I watched him in the rearview mirror as he pulled his head up from his phone.

"Yea, you should already know how we do when we put it down." His comment caught me off guard.

"What?" Jae twisted around in the seat, almost breaking my hand to give Trap a dirty look.

"Come on sis, I ain't tryna beef with you."

I wasn't going to interrupt because I knew Trap wouldn't disrespect Jae.

"Well, bruh, say how you feel." She snapped her neck. I knew the second that shit flew from Trap's mouth, she was going to be on his ass.

"I'm diggin' ya' sister, Jae."

"But you got a bitch in Atlanta." Her comeback was so strong and fast that I had to look over at her.

"That shit ain't saying nothing. That shit can't compare to what me and Chessan had created." That nigga sounded like me when I first met Jae. I couldn't get her out of my mind, no matter how far back I tried to push her.

"Trap." She cleared her throat, and I knew what she was about to spit what was coming from deep down inside of her. "If she allows you in her life and you fuck it up, you already know how I get down!" Her mouth had a way of cutting through metal.

"Sis, I won't." He reached his hand up front for her to shake it.

She looked at it before she accepted it. If Trap fucked up, his ass was grass. He had given her his word, and he had to live up to it or die.

"Is that what ya' problem is?" I intervened in the dispute, looking over at Jae.

"No!" She snapped and I let that shit slide because I knew her hormones were getting the better of her. On top of that, her family had just bounced from the country. Minutes passed before she said another word. "I gotta reach out to my father." She stared at me, but I kept my eyes on the road. I was all ears.

"And?"

"I'm scared," she finally admitted.

"Why?"

I listened to her as she poured her heart out. Seeing my baby crying in front of Trap, I knew the shit was real and deep. She tried not to cry in front of anyone 'cause an emotion is a sign that the enemy can use to conquer you, which I always publicized to her.

"And I've always told you. You can confront the nigga, and if it ain't what you want to hear, we can dust him off or you can walk away." I meant that. The only people I was loyal to was her grandparents. They had taken their time to raise and love her. "Whatever your decision is, I'm with you on it."

"And I'm with you on that shit, bruh." Trap tossed in. That caused Jae to turn her frown into a smile.

At the end of the day, all we had was each other.

***

Seeing MooMoo and MiMi approaching the truck had me feeling like the greatest father in the world. I didn't understand why muthafuckas had children and never participated in their lives. My kids were my world beside Jae, the loyal ones to me and the streets. And I couldn't wait for Jae to find out how far she was and what she was having.

"Daddy!" They both screamed, seeing me walking to them.

"Uncle Trap!" MooMoo yelled. Trap was out the truck, yet Jae stayed behind.

"What's good with you, baby girl?" He leaned down and kissed her forehead.

"Just chilling."

"Good, keep it that way. MiMi what's good, beautiful?" He kissed her too.

"Nothing," she said, wrapping her hands around my waist. MooMoo was getting older so she didn't show me that much attention like she did when she was younger unless she wanted something.

Trap walked up to his mother and wrapped his arms around her. The love that he had for her was priceless. At the end of the day, Ms. Judith was our mother and father. She loved us more than she loved herself. We came first.

"Thanks, Ma." I stepped out of MiMi's hold to let my mother know how much I appreciated her, even though she didn't birth me.

"No problem." She pulled Trap to one side so she could hug me with her other arm.

This was my family. They were my blood. And I'll die protecting the ones that.

***

We stopped at Junior's Cheesecake to grab some food before we headed home as a family.

"Daddy, so we living with you for good, now?" MooMoo asked once we got back in the truck.

"Yea, I'ma talk to ya' mothers and see if we can work something out."

I knew La'Quinnta would be happy to be free to do whatever, but Ashanti had to prove a point. Especially since Jae had beat her ass, again.

"Okay," she responded. She knew the drama, 'cause she was old enough to.

"But don't worry about that, though. Daddy got this!"

I saw Jae reaching, but it was too late.

Boom!

CHAPTER 23
JAE

By the time I pulled my gun out, the driver's window had already shattered into a million pieces.

"What the fuck?" Rocket swerved the truck, keeping it from crashing into a dump truck.

Blocka. Blocka. Blocka. I was in the driver's seat, literally in Rocket's lap, busting my pistol back. *Blocka. Blocka. Blocka.* "Don't wreck this bitch!" I yelled at Rocket, 'cause I knew it was difficult for him to see over my body. I had punched the rest of the broken glass window all the way out so I could spit fire from my 9.

The car backed back behind us so I couldn't see it anymore. Muthafuckas thought we were slipping.

Boom!

Rocket snatched me back by my ponytail. "Is you fuckin' crazy, yo!" I felt his words as they bounced off his tongue.

I jumped into the back of the Suburban, only to find Trap's body covering the girls on the floor. I leaped over them and into the third row, only to feel a bullet whisk pass my ear, lodging into the front windshield. Thank God Trap had the kids under him. *Damn!*

The back window crumbled and I was staring eye to eye with the enemy. Rocket slammed on the brakes and the car crashed into the back of the truck. The impact dropped me, but I continued to spit venom from my trigger finger, hoping I had hit the muthafucka.

Bitch ass niggas kept coming. I was on my feet in seconds because I knew time was a thing I couldn't take back if I had gotten caught slippin'. When I bounced up, the car was empty.

"Trap!" Rocket called out. I could hear anger in his voice.

"Yo!"

"Ya'll good?" he asked, looking at his right hand man laying over his girls.

"Get us the fuck out of here!" I said, getting in their conversation.

"What?" He barked. "I'm not leaving you!"

"You don't have a choice!" I clapped back. "You're on probation! I rather have you gone than locked the fuck up! You're a felon, remember?"

"Jae!" His eyes were piercing my soul.

Trap got up, checking himself and the girls. People were gathering around us, inquiring if we were okay.

"Go, I got this! I'll be home." I was still thunderstruck about what had just happened.

***

As soon as the cab door closed that they had got in, the cops pulled up. Deep.

"Put the gun down!" They had their weapons drawn at me and I knew from watching the news that having a gun and being black could bedeath.

"Slowly!" They yelled out to me like I wasn't the victim here, so I did as I was told. Slowly.

Face down, on my stomach with the gun out of my hands, they rushed to my body like flies on a fresh batch of shit.

"She didn't do anything!" I heard someone yelling. "She didn't do a damn thing!"

"I'm pregnant," I shouted out so they would handle me with care.

Being black was a crime itself to send me away for life without question, but having a gun in my possession in a shoot-out was way fucking critical. I could fuck around and get the chair, so I played cool.

Hearing the cuffs clicked on my wrist made me sick to my stomach, and I felt the little bit of food that I had just ate coming up as they stood me on my feet. I took a deep breath, getting my thoughts the fuck together.

"She didn't do anything, wrong!" a person voiced.

"Who are you?" an officer asked the lady as they ushered me to the back of a squad car.

"I'm a citizen of this country!"

I almost started laughing when she said that shit.

They seated me in the back of the cruiser with the cuffs eating away at my skin. I watched two officers questioning the lady in front of me as two more pigs directed traffic around the crash. Two stood at the cruiser with their hands on their weapons, waiting for a reason to chalk line my ass.

"Could ya'll please cuff me to the front, or not make these bitches so damn tight?"

"Excuse me?" a black bald-headed officer asked me, knowing damn well he had heard what the fuck I said.

"Y'all got these bloodclath shits too fucking tight on me!"

They both just looked at me and continued talking like I hadn't said a word.

"And what the fuck you gonna charge me with?" I wanted to see if the muthafucker was going to repeat himself, but when he didn't, I got real hype. "Defending my muthafuckin' self, is that a charge?"

These sons of bitches had the audacity to take me to headquarters for questioning after I heard a few witnessed telling them that I was defending myself.

"But there's more, Ms. James!" The chief of the department said. I hadn't changed my last name to Wallace on my driver's license as of yet. He was just as mad as me.

"Mr.—" I'd forgotten what the fuck his name was. That shit wasn't important.

"Edition," he reminded me, sitting in the chair across from me.

"Whatever! I've been here for hours and my answers have been the same." I was getting madder as the seconds passed. "I was driving by myself when someone pulled up beside me and started shooting. No, I don't know who they were or what they looked like because I wasn't trying to wreck and kill myself. I did fire my weapon because I was scared for my life."

He studied my face, but I kept that shit the same way—unreadable. I wasn't a fucking snitch and I damn sure wasn't scared of no fucking human that bled just like me.

"My weapon is registered to me, and if it's registered to me, then I have all rights to use it to save my life. Am I correct?"

He leaned back in the chair, crossed his legs and licked his dry ass, ashy lips. Fucking crackers always trying to break a muthafucka down so they can sell their soul. Not me. I was still cuffed, but at least it was just one hand to the wooden table.

He sat up. "Ms. James, I know you're full of shit and you know you are, too."

I bat my eyes and smiled inside 'cause I knew they couldn't charge me with shit. They found the shell casings that Mayo had fired at me, so they knew that I was defending myself. "Truth be told, I don't give a fuck if you think I'm full of shit."

He laughed before he slammed his fist on the table.

"Really?" I questioned him, letting him know that shit didn't scare me at all.

"You're full of shit!"

I laughed when seeing his veins bulging out of his forehead. "Great!" I smiled. There was nothing that he could do to break me. Nothing.

After four fucking hours, they decided to let me go. Ms. Judith was sitting in the lobby with two Jewish men sitting on the opposites side of her.

"How are you feeling?" She greeted me with a hug like she hadn't seen me in years.

"Better, now that I'm free."

"Good. Let's go!"

***

Rocket had got in touch with Gotti, and he'd reached out to his lawyers to assist me, but I didn't need their help. I was smart enough to know what to say. They kept my gun, which was fine with me. A bitch always had extra ammo.

"Babe!" Rocket addressed me with a kiss when I walked through thefront door.

"Babi!" I kissed him back.

"The girls are worried about you."

"Where are they?"

Trap was smoking a blunt on the sofa with a bottle of 1800 in his hand. "Sleep."

"Good."

Ms. Judith said goodbye and I thanked her once again for showing up to get me. "Anything for y'all."

I explained everything to Rocket, right there in the living room, inhaling the loud pack that Trap was puffing on.

"What address you gave them?" Rocket asked.

"Shit, I didn't give them one. They made a copy of my license. The old address is on that bitch."

"Oh, okay." He got up, picking the Mac 11 up front the side of the sofa.

ROCKET

Mufuckas lived by the pistol, so they, or the ones they love, are gonna die by that bitch.

"Where you going?" Jae asked, looking at my outfit from head to toe.

"You already know." I kissed her forehead.

Trap sat the 1800 bottle on the table, dropping the rest of the blunt in the ashtray. My nigga was ready. He lived for this shit just like I did. I knew Jae wanted to go by the way her face was looking, but she had to stay here and hold down the fort.

"You already know if you need me, just—"

I cut her off. "I already know, Mrs. Wallace." I kissed her lips one last time before I tucked the .45 in my waist. The Mac 11 was over my shoulders already.

I knew that nigga Mayo wasn't about that life, and I had a feeling Cuba put fire under his ass to make that move that he did earlier.

Gotti had got me a low-key whip to travel in tonight, just like a ghost.

Trap was silent, but I knew that nigga was thinking. When the shooting took place earlier, he told me, "Them niggas lucky my nieces were inside, 'cause you already know, bruh." I knew what he meant. He would've chased them mufuckas down on foot, blazing in broad daylight, not giving a fuck about anything.

"Hit 'am where it's gonna hurt, Rocket," my father's words played over and over in my head. "Mufuckas didn't give a fuck if they had touched ya' girls, so don't spare a soul, animals included!" I ran the shit down to OX, even though I knew what I had to do just to hear his opinion. "Let that muthafucka bow to his knees at ya' gangsta, son!"

My blood was still boiling from earlier, knowing that my seeds had got caught up in the blazing, but they were chill about it. I asked them not to mention it to their mothers and they both agreed that it was our secret.

"My nigga, you ready?" I parked the car around the block, pulling my face mask down and adjusting the black gloves on my hands.

"Bruh, when you know me not to be ready?" Trap asked me, checking the banana clip for the AK 47.

"Say no more." I left the car running with the lights off.

The street was as quiet as a morgue as we moved. The Mac 11 felt so good in my hands that I couldn't wait to hear it talk. I tried to find a latch to open the gate, but I couldn't find one. So, I jumped over the baby gate like a Rottweiler. Trap followed suit. We circled around the house to see if we were lucky to come up on an open window or door, but that bitch luck wasn't on our side.

Boom!

I kicked the back door but it didn't budge, so I kicked it again twice by the knob, and bingo. It opened. The Mac 11 paved the way for me as I entered a part of the house. Seeing the time on a microwave blinking, let me know that I was in the kitchen.

A light turned on, so we stopped walking.

"Castro," a female voice called out. "Castro!" The voice was getting closer and closer to us.

An old lady turned the corner and she got face to face with my Mac.

"Arggh!"

I knocked her old ass in the temple, sending her body flying to the floor.

Trap closed the back door the best he could as I stepped over her body.

"Grandma?" I ran into a little boy, no older than six. "Where is my grandma?" he asked, scared to death. His body was shaking uncontrollably.

"Shut the fuck up!" Trap pointed the hammer at his trembling lip.

Tears danced down his innocent face.

"Stay posted my nigga!" I left Trap with the victims while I searched the house, hoping I would find my prey. But the muthafucka wasn't there.

When I got back to the kitchen, Cuba's mother was wide awake. Trap had cracked the refrigerator door so we could see. He had her and the little boy sitting in the corner of the kitchen with the 47 pointed at them.

The old lady held the little boy to her chest, tight.

"Where is Castro?" I asked, bending down in front of them. Castro was Cuba's first name.

She hugged the little boy tighter, trying to protect him. She had yet to answer me.

"Huh?"

"If I knew where he was, I wouldn't tell you!" Her allegiance to her son was compact. The lady went harder than a lot of niggas in the streets. I respected her answer, but I damn sure didn't respect her tone.

I stood to my feet and smiled.

Blocka. Blocka. Blocka.

The .45 took her face off. Her hands dropped from holding the little boy as her body slumped to the side. The little boy's eyes got big, but he didn't scream or holler. He just stared up at me with blood all over his face. He was in shock. I didn't have it in me to kill an innocent child, so I headed to the door. The little nigga didn't see my face.

Boom. Boom. Boom.

I didn't turn around to see what I knew happened.

CHAPTER 24
JAE

I took a real quick, hot shower to get the precinct's funky scent the fuck up off of me. Then, I prayed to God to watch over Rocket and Trap. The pandemonium from earlier had me out the shower and dressed within minutes. I paced the house with a ready to fire Glock 40 in my right hand and a .38 special in my left hand, watching and waiting for Rocket and Trap to return. I had checked in on the girls and they were still sleeping. My nerves had me worrying. Seeing the window shattered today had me frightened, still. I couldn't sit down with that image in my head. I kept checking the security monitors to see if I saw anything out of order outside of the house. Everything seemed peaceful.

"Come on, Rocket," I whispered to myself in the dark as I continued to pace. There was no way in hell that I could close my eyes without Rocket and Trap in this house. "Fuck!"

As the time ticked away, the more I started to think that the worse had taken place. I took a seat in front of the blunt that Trap had left in the ashtray. I needed something to calm my fucking nerves. I figured the 1800 would be bad since I was pregnant, so I picked the spliff up. *Bad but not as bad.*

I dropped the blunt on the floor when seeing the sensor light going the fuck off on the monitor. I pulled the hammer back on the .38, waiting to finger fuck the trigger. The .40 was waiting, ready to send a bloodclath intruder back out the door.

The light stopped flashing as I studied the monitors.

"Jae?"

I jumped, seeing MooMoo standing beside me with her eyes on the guns in my hands.

"Yes," I responded in a tremulous voice, looking away from the screens.

"Are you okay?"

I put my attention back on the screens. "Yes, I'm okay. Why you asked?"

"Because you are shaking," she said, walking away from me to take a seat on the love set.

I glanced down at my hands to check them out, and as she said, I was shaking. My left foot danced under me, but it wasn't from nerves or fear. It was my protective side ready to strike whoever that thought they could run up in this bitch.

"Daddy." I heard the love in Moo's voice for her father, and I turned around to find Rocket and Trap coming up from the basement.

"That damn baby gonna come out a fucking trapper!" Trap expressed with his silly self, and I cracked a smile. Deep down inside I was glowing; happy to have my man back home with me. *Thank you, Lord.*

"Why you up, Moo?"

"She was keeping me company," I answered for her, and she smiled.

Rocket's outfit was still flawless, but there was no way I could spot blood on black, so I checked his feet out to find nothing.

"Go back to sleep, baby girl." Rocket walked over and kissed her forehead.

Mo disappeared from the room to hers upstairs. Trap left us standing there after he got his drink and blunt off the floor.

"Been to sleep?" Rocket asked me.

I inserted the .40 in the back of my shorts, looking up at the man that had my soul. "I couldn't without you in this house, or our bed."

***

As always, I bagged up his dirty clothes while he took a shower. After that, I headed to bed to wait on him to grace his spot beside me, where he belonged.

"Tomorrow, I gotta check in with my PO." I heard Rocket's voice, but I was too damn tired to answer him. His hand gripped my ass, and my pussy literally jumped, bringing me out of my sleep.

I had fallen asleep waiting on him. "I know. Have you figured out how you was going to handle the situation with the girls' mothers?" I rolled over to sink my face into his chest under his chin.

"No, not really."

I knew he was more worried about knocking Cuba's head off. Plus, finshing Ro's father along with Mayo, and finding a leader for JMoney's old spot, he didn't have time to worry about his babies' mothers.

"I touched Cuba's heart, tonight, though."

"Huh?" I twined my legs with his as I rubbed his washboard abs.

"I knocked his mother and son off."

"What?" I lifted my head up off his chest, but it was too dark for me to see into his eyes.

He cuffed my neck, bringing me back down. I was shocked when hearing that he'd rocked a female and a child to sleep, but witnessing Mayo shooting at us with the girls in the truck must've been the ice-breaker for him.

"I didn't have the heart to rock the little boy." Even with all the shit he'd been through, he still had a heart. A pure one. "But Trap—"

I cut him off. I knew Trap didn't give a fuck about a child's life. He was what the streets made him. A monster, like me. Anyone that crossed the line and tried to take mine out or hurt them, had it coming from me, straight like that. Baby, man, woman, or animal, even a fucking fly.

"That's why you need me with you. What you can't complete, I'll do it for you."

I knew he was smiling. "Jae," he whispered in the sexiest voice ever.

"Yes."

"Make me tap out."

The realest nigga alive only had to tell me once. I moved my head towards his dick, licking my lips as my pussy began to pulsate.

ROCKET

Fuck! I rubbed my eyes before extending my hand, reaching for Jae, but she wasn't in the bed. The digital dash on the cable box display that it was 7:28AM. *Damn!* I jumped out of the bed, grabbing my boxers up off of the carpet and throwing them on, before I got a pair of jeans and a black t-shirt to throw on my body. Jae damn sure made a nigga curl the fuck up with the way she tossed the pussy to me last night. Her pussy was that from the gate, but ever since she got pregnant, that muthafucka was the truth. I couldn't even remember shit else after I busted up in that joint.

"Babe!" I yelled, coming out of our bedroom, putting my NY fitted on.

"I'm in here!" she shouted.

I chased the accent like a crackhead chased the dope man.

The girls were dressed and ready for school. My baby girls were getting big, fast. I smiled at Jae because she had gotten up and made sure my babies were ready to face the day.

"I was going to let you sleep in," she chuckled.

I shot her that *I got you later* look.

"Daddy, we are going to be late!" MiMi said, sounding just like her mother. I prayed that's the only trait that she'd have of that bitch.

"I know. Let's go." I sent Trap a quick text, letting him know that we were leaving, then I activated the alarm system.

***

After dropping the girls off of at school, I called my PO and told her I was on my way to pay her a visit. This was my first time seeing her in her office since the shooting.

"How are you feeling, Mr. Wallace?" She met me in the waiting room.

"I've had better days, but I can't complain. I'm breathing, and that's a lot to give thanks for."

"Yes," she agreed, but she could never understand the world that I was facing head on. "Follow me." She talked with her hand.

I closed the door the moment I was in her office.

"Take a seat." She walked behind her desk, moving the mouse around to her computer before she took a seat.

She had a few degrees hanging on the wall, along with a family portrait. She had a boy and a girl. The man in the picture was black.

"Sorry about your losses." She tapped the keyboard. "I got a report stating that you were present at the service and the burial."

I leaned back in the chair, waiting for her to make eye contact with me.

"Have the police contacted you about the shooting that claimed your mother's life?" When she looked at me, I saw concern in her eyes, but that bullshit didn't flatter me. That bitch mother of mine got exactly what she had coming to her.

"Thank you." I had to play the game right. "No, no one took the time to reach out to me." I kept my eyes on hers.

"It's crazy, but I know they are working hard on the case."

"Do they have a lead?" I didn't give a fuck, I just wanted to see what she knew.

She faced the screen of the computer. "I'm not sure, but I know they can't say you had anything to do with it."

I was glad that Jae had her brothers to do the job for me. Damn, I fuckin' love that girl. I was clear of that shit because of her.

"Witnesses came forth saying that you were running for your life like everyone else."

"It's hard but it's going to be fine," I said, playing the hurt role.

She didn't respond right away, but typed something. "How are you coping?" She leaned back in her chair.

"I'm living, spending time with my girls." I let that sink in before I kept going. "I'm making up for the time that I missed."

She smiled. "Well, since your brother is deceased, I have no choice but to take you off papers."

It was my turn to smile. She came forth in the chair and moved the mouse, clicking away. Seconds later, a few pieces of paper came out of her printer. She reached over and removed them, placing them in front of me.

Before signing anything, I made sure I read it word for word. The document made it clear that I had completed my probation successfully.

"Thank you," I said, exiting her office and building for good.

***

"Hit Eastern Parkway, babe." Jae was on her phone when I got back to the car.

She nodded as she shifted the car into drive. "Yuh a sumting else." Whoever she was talking to had to be Jamaican, 'cause she was speaking in her language. "Mi luv yuh, tu," she said, ending the call. "What happened?" She asked, touching my hand.

"She took me off papers."

"Really?"

I gave her the details about the meeting that I'd had. "Thanks for planning that shit out for me."

"You know having ya' back in life is my number one goal."

"I know!" Once we were on Eastern Parkway, I directed her with my hand. "Park between the truck and the minivan, babe."

When she parked, she glanced up at the sign and smiled at me.

CHAPTER 25
JAE

"You strapped?"

"Yea." He lifted his shirt up so I could see the hammer.

"Good." I moved the .40 from under my leg and put it under my seat. Pussyclath pigs had took my strap but that didn't stop me from being strapped. I'ma die with one in my hand. "I'd be damned to be far away from one."

"I already know."

I opened the door and he followed.

"When you planned this?"

"Shit kept coming up so I had Ms. Judith make you an appointment," he said, holding the door for me to enter the doctor's office.

"Hello," an older white lady welcomed us at the front desk.

"Hello. I have an appointment." Rocket squeezed my ass.

"Name,lease?"

"Jae Ja—" I stopped, remembering that I was married. "Jae Wallace."

"Okay, Mrs. Wallace, take a seat and the doctor will be with you in a few."

"Thank you." Rocket answered for me.

The waiting room was empty and I wondered if Rocket had paid extra for that to happen.

"I want a boy," he said, picking up a baby magazine as he sat beside me.

"I don't care what I'm having. As long as it healthy, I'm good."

"I know it's a boy, though." He was flipping through the pages as I watched Bold and The Beautiful. That show been playing since I was a little girl in Jamaica.

"How you figure?" I faced him.

"'Cause I was doing all the work when I came home." He had to laugh at his own damn joke because he knew I wasn't a lazy fuck.

"You ain't did no work last night." I laughed in his ear.

"You ain't saying nothing, baby."

"Mrs. Wallace, come this way," the old lady said, interrupting our conversation.

"I bet it's a boy." Rocket slapped my ass in front of the lady.

Her face got beet red and I couldn't help but to smile.

"Bet!"

She escorted us to a room down the hall and opened the door for us to enter. "There is a gown on the examination table. Put it on and the doctor will be in with you." She left us in the room alone.

Rocket took a seat to the far right in the corner, eyeing me down. "Let me taste it."

"What?"

"Let me taste it."

"Now?" I was taken back by his request.

"Yea."

I took my clothes off and wrapped myself up in the gown that was on the table, then walked over to my man, bending over to grab my ankles in front of him.

When he flicked his tongue across my ass, I stumbled forward but his hands were fast and he gripped me by the waist before licking my cookie.

"Rocket," I purred, arching my back and touching my toes. My thugga was a freak. His tongue circled my clit. I grabbed my feet. Then, he stopped and laughed. "What the fuck?" I snapped, looking back at him to find a smile on his face as he licked his full lips. "Why you—"

In came the doctor with his assistant. "I'm Dr. Douglas." He reached his hand out and I took it.

"I'm Jae. Jae Wallace, and this is my husband." I was heated at Rocket for having my pum pum jumping like a kangaroo.

"Take a seat so we can get started."

I sat on the table and mean mugged Rocket for the stunt he'd pulled. He looked at me and licked his lips. The doctor and his assistant washed their hands before they put gloves on.

"When was your last period?" Dr. Douglas asked.

"I'm not sure."

"Estimate?"

"About three months ago, I think." Rocket had been home for almost five months now.

"Don't worry, we'll find out. Go ahead and lay back."

I felt uncomfortable having another man touching my body. When his hands touched my leg, I tensed the fuck up.

"Just relax," he said.

Rocket read my face and got up and stood beside me, holding my hand. "Relax, babe, I got you."

The assistant, a female, opened my gown, exposing my stomach. She spread a gel over my stomach and stepped out the way so the doctor could do his job.

"This is an ultrasound. With this, we'll see and measure the baby." He pointed to the monitor off to the side of us with the scope on my stomach.

When I glanced at the screen, I saw my baby. Tears sprung to my eyes instantly. My heart raced as emotions got the best of me. I was already in love. Rocket pecked my forehead. This wasn't new to him but it was to me. Joy, happiness, peace, everything good found me, and my heart melted. It wasn't just me anymore. I had a little one to protect, to love, and care for till air left my body. I wondered how my mother could've left me when she saw me inside of her.

"You're three months. That means your due date will be in February."

My tears kept running. They were happy ones. I wasn't upset at Rocket anymore. Because of his freaky ass, I was getting the greatest gift ever. Being a mother.

"When will we find out what we're having?" Rocket questioned the doctor as I stared at the display, still bathing and soaking in the moment.

"In two months, but I need to see her every month to make sure everything is okay."

Rocket wiped my tears away, but they found their way back. The doctor pressed a button and I heard, "*thump, thump, thump*." I took a deep breath. I knew what it was. It was my baby's heart beating.

"That's a great sound."

Hearing, seeing and knowing that I had an angel inside of me made me the happiest person on earth.

"I love you." I looked up at my husband. "Thanks." I was scared to death to be without him.

"I love you, too, and thank you."

ROCKET

We made another appointment after Jae had her blood drawn. The assistant informed us that if anything was to go wrong at anytime, call 911 or rush to the nearest emergency room, then contact them.

Jae was still basking in the moment, so I took the wheel over.

"That little nigga gonna be just like me, you heard?" I was praying for a boy. I was going to build the bond that I yearned to have with my father with my little nigga.

"I already know, babi." She grabbed my leg. "I've got to call Wilber."

"Whatever decision that you come up with towards ya' father, know that I'ma rock with you."

"I know you will."

***

Jae dropped that mushy shit the second I turned to hit the projects that JMoney ran. My bitch G'd the fuck up on command in seconds, reaching under the seat to retrieve her burner.

"Who you gonna let run this shit?"

"Whoever you pick!" When I was banged up, she was around, so I trusted her decision. So, when she gave me her answer, I had to agree.

Niggas were in attendance when I got to the meeting spot. They were looking at me like I was a ghost. The table had about twenty chairs around it with the head chair empty.

"You wanna sit down?" I asked Jae.

"Naw, you go ahead. I'ma stand right here."

Niggas were watching our interaction closely.

As I stepped towards the table, I studied each and every single niggas' face, trying to pick up on any disloyalty. JMoney's right hand man had his chair beside the empty one. Fuck taking a seat, I stood behind the chair with my hands on it.

"Where is JMoney?" I looked at Scarface.

"The nigga has been missing for days." He paused, looking down at the table. "We found his car, empty. Phone calls going straight to his voicemail." He brought his head up, locking his eyes on me. "That shit is crazy, 'cause he ain't ever did no shit like this before." He sounded like someone had plunged a dagger into his back. He was hurting for their leader, but his leader had an outbreak of diarrhea at the mouth.

"If a muthafucka can't be silent about the simple things, how do you expect him to keep quiet about a hurricane?" Those were my wife's words, and she made hell sense.

"But the show must go on!" His statement was as straight as an arrow. "Niggas still gotta eat, muthafuckas." He waved his hand around the table. "Muthafuckas got families to feed, so we can't let that shit tear us down."

I pulled the chair out, placing my right foot in the seat. My .45 was poking me in my side, so I removed it from my waist and placed it on the table. I saw Jae touching her side and I knew she was holding the handle to hers. She stayed on point.

"Okay." I acknowledged his words. "Well, as of today, Scarface, you are in charge."

He stretched back in the chair, taking in what I had just said.

"Run this muthafucker with loyalty. Treat the crew with love. There is money to be made. A lot of it, so everyone can be straight."

Niggas smiled.

"That I can do," Scarface said, looking at his crew.

That's all I needed to hear. I cleared the room, leaving just Scarface and Jae present at the table. Scarface pulled a duffle bag out from between his legs and sat it on the table.

"What's that?"

"Seven hundred and fifty thousand." He pushed the bag over to me. "The thirty bricks that Jae gave us."

I pushed the bag back over to him. "Spread that shit equally between the crew."

His face was priceless. I needed this nigga to know that I respected the hustle and the hard work that the team had done for my empire.

"Treat ya' soldiers like you would want to be treated. Never give them the opportunity to get jealous of you, because they'll cross you. Show them you appreciate all that they do, and their loyalty will lie with you forever!" OX had schooled me over the jack phone he had.

I dapped the nigga up before I left the room with Jae in front of me.

***

"My little nigga." I embraced Goon, nothing 'bout this nigga was little but his age.

"My nigga." He dapped me up, smiling from ear to ear. "You got more lives than a fuckin' cat, yo." I leveled my eyes on him. "When I get older, I wanna be just like you!"

"You gotta be built like me from the sack, lil' nigga," I said, walking into the building.

"Outta a few, I'm one of those real niggas, too!"

I watched Jae's ass jiggle in front of me as I listened to Goon. His character had shown me that from the first day.

"Niggas wanna act like they 'bout that life, but they ain't! Me? I'm all the way 'bout that!"

I was seated at the card table with my OG, Killa, behind the walls when I saw the crowd by the phone getting bigger. It was Goon who stared down six niggas who was trying to punk him that day. He was the one to start that brawl that had our asses on lockdown. Lil' nigga had heart and balls of a lion. Nigga came back from isolation and ended up in the room with Killa's friend, and just like that, we clicked. It was right I put him on when he touched down.

"Shit ain't been the same, Rocket."

I took a seat in his studio apartment. Jae sat beside me. The niggas he lost were family. I knew what he was going through. I had been through it when Tray die.

"Shit ain't been the same, but the money still flowing." He took a seat, too. "It's just me and Brad."

It was four of them together. They grew up together like I did with Tray and Trap. "Yea, we hurting, but we still trapping."

I saluted the lil nigga's motto for not allowing one problem to turn into two.

"How are the familes?" Jae asked, showing her soft side.

"They good, you know. Mourning, but they straight. As long as I'm alive, they gonna be good, and my niggas' names will stay alive." He raised his hands, showing me the back of his arms. His tats read: *RIP SKIP* and *RIP BLACK.*

His loyalty and love for his niggas reminded me of myself. I had stopped by Ms. Judith's spot before I made my way over here.

"I wanna be a part of that nigga's party that did my niggas in." His poisonous remark showed me what he preached from day one. He was about that life.

"Say no more."

His eyes watered and I knew he was hurting. There's nothing worse than losing the ones that you love. Court was going to be held in the streets fa' sho'.

I tossed the bag at his feet. "That's a little something for the families. I won't be in attendance for the funerals, but Jae will be. Keep an eye out for her."

I didn't want her to go, but once her mind was made up, I couldn't change it.

"That ain't nothing for you to ask me to do." Goon expressed.

Me and this lil' nigga was cut from the same cloth. *Realness.*

CHAPTER 26
JAE

Going to bed late and getting up early had me tired, so I let Rocket know how I was feeling the moment we got back in the car.

"Aite," he said, rubbing my stomach. "My boy whooping that ass, I see."

"Whatever." I leaned my upper body back in the seat with my .40 in my hand, resting it by my pussy. "If it's a girl, yo ass gonna be sick." I laughed.

"I'm telling you it's a boy, yo."

"Aite." I closed my eyes as his free hand massaged my stomach.

***

"Babe, we home." Rocket woke me up in the driveway.

"What you 'bout to do?" I questioned him, sitting up and wiping saliva from the side of my mouth.

The front door opened and Trap emerged from the house with a black hood covering his head.

"We gonna check all the spots out."

Trap stood outside the car, waiting and giving us some privacy as he answered his phone.

"Aite, I love you." I leaned over and let our lips rock.

"I love you, more." Rocket delivered to me the second I pulled away.

"And brush ya' teeth," he cracked up.

The little cat nap that I took in the car had me re-energize. So much shit had been going on to the point that I deprived myself of sleep, so I've just been getting it when I could to function.

"Damn," I said out loud, looking at the missed calls on my phone. There was four to be exact.

I pulled the .40 from my waist and sat it on the table in the kitchen so I could grab a bottle of cranberry juice from the fridge.

"Hello!" I snapped, answering my phone without looking to see who it was.

"Wah a gwan?"

I pulled the iPhone from my ear to look at the number that had an 876 area code. Jamaica. "Mi deh yah," I answered the caller, opening the bottle.

"Yuh know ow yuh a chat tu?" They wanted to know if I knew who I was talking to.

"Of course, I do." I took a sip from the container in my hand. "Wilber, my father." Sarcasm echoed in my voice.

"Jae, I really don't know where to start." He stopped as I swallowed some of the juice.

"Start at the beginning. You could do that!" I spoke like I was the one that gave birth to him.

He took a deep, long breath before he said a word. "I love you, no matter how you feel." His words cut so deep that I had to take a seat.

So many years had passed for him just to tell me that he loved me. I choked up just hearing those words that I've dream of. He had the floor, so there was no need to interfere.

"Out of all my children, you didn't let my lack of love break or demolish you."

He didn't know how many nights I soaked my pillow, just wishing our relationship was different. I didn't understand that he was supposed to be the second man in my life instead of my grandfather, 'cause God was first. He didn't know that I chased love because I didn't get it from him, even though my grandfather loved me the best that he could. Tears splashed on the glass table in front of me.

"I remember the day you left Jamaica." I heard him sniffle. "I tried so hard not to break down, but I couldn't. When your mother left you, I didn't know what to do. I had to drop you off at my mother's house." He sighed with relief.

"It wasn't their responsibility to raise me, daddy." This was my first time calling him that word in years. "It wasn't." I exhaled, remembering that I was breathing for two.

"Jae, I know. It's not like I didn't know how to care for you. I was just scared that I wouldn't do a good job."

I smiled through my tears, listening to him admitting his flaws to me.

"They did an amazing job raising you. Look how you turned out."

For two hours, I talked to my father. I cried and I laughed, I laughed and I cried as we opened up to each other about things that were eating away at our souls. We were the same sign— Virgo. His birthday was the first and mine was the sixth. We both were as stubborn as a rock. I told him about Rocket, our wedding, and me being pregnant. He was happy that I was happy and couldn't wait to meet my husband.

"Have you talked to your mother?"

I hadn't talked to her in years, and I didn't want to. She knew better. She'd carried me for nine months inside of her. "No!" I was getting mad just thinking about why she left me.

"Do you want to?"

I let his words flow for a minute. "Daddy, I'm good. If she reaches out, then okay. If not, I'm still going to be okay."

"When you going to visit Jamaica?" he asked, changing the subject.

I promised him that I would visit soon before we said our goodbyes. Today so far, had turned out to be a beautiful day after all. I burned Rocket's and Trap's clothes, cleaned the house, took a shower and hit the sheets, smiling.

ROCKET

Even though the production warehouse was under control and running smoothly, I still had to show my face once in a while so mufuckas didn't get the wrong idea floating around in their heads.

"I replaced that nigga JMoney with his right hand man, Scarface."

Trap's attention was on the traffic all around us. The other day was a close call for all of us. So, his precaution level was on high alert. "That's a boss move you made, B."

"Yea, Jae told me how that nigga explained to her how we caught Ro before shit got to the boys."

"Hell yeah. Shit could've been looking ugly for us right now if it wasn't for that nigga's setup."

I didn't want the attention of the Feds, so I was glad that nigga got murked before he started his assignment. Working for the system. The system didn't have to do shit when it came to the streets. Confidential informants did the work for them. A muthfucka got jammed up, and instead of doing the time, they'd rather tell on the next. Not me.

I parked the car in the parking lot under the building. "You talked to Chessan?" We were in the elevator, heading up to the 28th floor.

My nigga was smiling from ear to ear when I brought up Jae's sister's name. "Every day, bruh. Everyday."

"How you feeling 'bout that?" I fixed my jeans. The strap wasn't positioned right.

"Man, I think I'm in love."

"Fuck outta here!" I got excited for my dawg. "No, not you, in love." I tried to check his forehead to make sure he wasn't running a fever, but he smacked my hand away, laughing.

"Yo, them island women is the truth."

"You ain't gotta tell me." Jae had shown me that the second I met her, and I knew I had to have her. Years later and she was still mine.

Bing. The elevator stopped. I pulled my cell phone out, hitting a few buttons as we were exiting the small space.

"I'm here." I said into the phone, then ended the call.

Click. Clack. Click. Clack.

The sound of the bolts unlocking was like music to my ears. "What's good, son?"

The door opened and there stood Gotti. My father said it was best that Gotti handled the production department while I did the distribution part. "Breathing." He stepped to the side, allowing me and Trap to enter.

Usually niggas would be standing over the twenty stoves that was in there, but not today. Today, the only thing visible was a table where two heavy built Hispanic males were sitting.

"Greetings," I said, taking a seat.

Trap played the background scene as Gotti sat on my side.

"Hola," one of them spoke as the other acknowledged me with a small head nod.

"Nice to finally meet you, Rocket." He figured he was the man in charge. His English wasn't great, but I understood what he was trying to get across to me. Money didn't have an accent.

"Good and you?" I rubbed my hands together, ready to talk business.

My father had planned this meeting the day he found out that the slugs hadn't sent me away.

"Your father and I have been doing business for years." He was the only connect my father ever had. "We aim towards the same color— green— but we stand on loyalty as the foundation."

Gotti sat back in the chair. My fingers were locked together on top of the table. If this was just another nigga preaching about loyalty to me, I would've shut that shit down. But this was the connect, my father's acquaintance, my bread and butter.

"OX suggested that our connection had to be made because he was getting old," he chuckled. "But I told him, money gets old, but the value is still the same."

I had to nod and crack a half a smile so he wouldn't think that he was boring me to death.

"My point is this: I don't have a son to pass the torch down to. But he does. I'll continue to supply you with whatever you need as long as you're loyal to me."

The nigga beside him pulled a gold pistol from his side and placed it on the table. I did the same. Only difference was mine was black. I didn't have to look back at Trap to know that my nigga had his hand on the handle of his. The nigga had his goon and I had mine, but I was a shooter myself.

He smiled and Gotti kicked my leg with his foot. This Hispanic mufucka wasn't going to sit here and try to intimidate me in my spot, in my borough. He'd better pick his next words correctly or his brains were gone be left sitting at the table. Plug or not.

"I know you're moving a hundred bricks a month."

"Correct, but I could do more," I said.

"Say the number."

"Probably two." There were times that we had to wait for a shipment to come through so we were missing out on money. I wanted a constant flow.

"The price won't be the same." This was the first time that he took his eyes off me.

"Whatever you name, I can do. As long as the product stays the same." I fixed my hat with my left hand, showing him the same respect.

Discussing the numbers were easy. Since I wanted more, he had to pay more to get it to me, so I understood exactly where he was coming from. We shook hands once everything was cleared up and ready to be in motion.

"Gotti, I'ma holla at you later."

"Be easy, young goon," he responded.

I moved to the door with Trap at my side, only to stop before I unlocked the door.

"Mi amigo."

I looked back at the plug. "Loyalty isn't something you have to preach to me. I was born with it and I'll die standing on it."

***

"You was almost plugless just now, yo," said Trap as we dipped from Fulton Street.

My nigga's loyalty was unmatchable and I didn't have to pay him for it.

"Who you telling?" I was thinking the same thing when his boy pulled the hammer out.

"Nigga think just because he's in a position to supply that he can't be touched or replaced."

I was mad at what the connect had done, but Trap was heated. We wasn't blood, but our loyalty to each other made us thicker than blood.

After dropping in on every trap of mine, I decided to pick my girls up from school.

"How Lil' Trap doing?" I asked Trap as were waiting.

"Lil' nigga getting big. Talking 'bout how he love the A more than New York."

"What the fuck?" I had to laugh.

"Same thing I said, bruh. But his ass 'bout to come back to the Big Apple."

"How come?"

"I can't fuck with shorty up there when my heart is in the UK."

I had to look at the nigga real good, but I heard the seriousness in his voice.

JAE

"Ayo, fuck all that shit you sayin'!"

I woke up to Rocket standing in the middle of the room, watching me with the phone to his ear.

"So, you saying, if I don't bring MiMi back, you going to file a missing person's report?"

I sat up in the bed, rubbing my temple ,trying to put together the conversation that Rocket was having with his dumb ass egg carrier.

"You gonna tell the police I kidnapped my own child?" Rocket's composure was unruffled, but I knew deep down inside, he was fuming. His fucking brother had involved the police in their beef, and because of that, the nigga was six feet under, and here he was going through some police shit with Ashanti. He continued listening to her but I could tell that he was planning something vicious for her with the way his eyebrows arched. "Really, yo?" He seemed confused to what she had just said. "I know you'd rather have me in jail, than on the streets. This I know. But why?"

He'd never bad-mouthed his kids' mothers to me, he just wasn't that type of a nigga. I had to see these bitch's true colors myself for me to recognize who they truly were.

"But I don't want to be with you!" He sat on the bed in front of me.

I moved forward and took the phone from his ear. He let go without a fight.

"What we had was supposed to be for a lifetime! That bitch ain't shit! What can she do that I can't do? Huh, Rocket?" She was yelling.

"Ashanti," I spoke, and I heard her gasped for air. "First of all, don't disrespect me or mine." I bet she was shocked to hear me on the phone. "That police shit that you spitting is a no-no." I had yet to raise my voice at her.

"Jae, this ain't ya' fucking business!" She screamed.

"Anything that goes on with Rocket is my business." I let the hoe know. I was getting pissed the fuck of the more I heard her breathing. "I don't want to beef." I was trying to defuse the problem before it got too far. "Can we talk this out like women?"

"When?" She snapped.

"Friday."

"Bring my daughter when you come."

"We'll see you Friday, Ashanti." I ended the call, dropping the phone on the bed.

I took Rocket's hat off and tossed in on the carpet. I knew he wanted that bitch dead, but he didn't want his daughter to go insane. He was between a rock and a hard place. Family was everything to me. They're who I lived for and who I'd die for. I'd murder a brick and kill a rock about mine. That bitch wasn't related to me, so fuck her. She just made it easier for me to murk that ass.

I kissed Rocket's ear. "How was ya' day?" I whispered as my tongue danced inside his ear.

"You want me to tell you now, or when I'm tearing that pussy open." His voice made my box wet.

"You can tell me anything when you tearing this pussy up." I mounted him cow girl style, locking my legs behind him.

"Well, let me get to work then," he said, pulling his dick out and pushing it all the way up in me.

He fucked me so damn good while he told me about the meeting that had taken place between him and the plug. When he told me that he'd pulled his pistol out on the nigga, I busted all over him. His gangsta alone had me gone and I couldn't help but to bow down to his dick and his gangsta.

CHAPTER 27
ROCKET

Today's the little goons service and I knew I said I wasn't going to attend, but the way shit was right now between me and Cuba, I decided to travel with Jae and Trap. Business could wait. I had to pay my respects to the generals and made sure I was around to protect my wife and my brother, just in case shit popped off.

"How yuh feeling, babi?" Jae asked me. We were sitting in the back row of the church, but I didn't respond. I just squeezed her hand.

Trap was sitting to the left of her.

"Today, we are gathered here to pay respect to God's children." The pastor said, opening up the ceremony. "Let us bow our heads."

He continued but I didn't comply. I had to be on point. Jae's eyes were wide open, and her head was up. Trap's eyes were looking all over the church.

I spotted Goon and the other general at the door, scanning the room. Goon had acknowledged me with a solute, only for me to return one. Nothing but dope niggas were in attendance. Respect was given when it was earned, and from the amount of people there, I knew the dead ones were well respected.

Once the service was over, everyone was given another chance to say goodbye to the soldiers. As I made my way up front, Jae made her way to the grieving parents.

Looking into the caskets, I realized how crazy life was. One minute you're here and the next you're gone.

"Niggas gave their lives to the game, from day one." I knew Goon's voice from anywhere, so I didn't turn around.

"But the game ain't gonna be right 'til that muhfucka is dead!"

Both Skip and Black looked peaceful. They were dressed just like they did when they were alive— fresh white tee's, fitted hats with the CH logo, a diamond stud earring and a thick gold chain.

"I already know," I said, stepping out of the way so the next person could pay their respects.

"Good, 'cause a nigga can't sleep 'til that shit is handled."

I dapped him up. "Don't worry, you'll be a part of that nigga's going away party, fam."

"Say no more." He released me.

The church was clearing out. Jae was hugging the mothers when shit went from zero to a hundred in the blink of an eye. Bullets rained inside the church like a snowstorm as I made a dash to cover up Jae.

She and the parents were on the aisle when I tried to protect them by spitting back. Lil' Goon had yet to move. The nigga was acting like he was invisible. The two P89's in his hands had him feeling untouchable.

Seconds passed that felt like hours before the shooting stopped. Screams exploded from everywhere. I jumped up on my feet to see Trap standing over a nigga's body at the front door.

Blocka. Blocka. BLocka. He fucked the trigger of the gat into the person's chest.

I saw Lil' Goon go down on his knees and I ran to his side. "You bleeding," I said, looking at the blood all over his white tee shirt.

"I—" His eyes closed. "I know." Just as quickly, his eyes flickered back open.

I pulled my white tee over my body and applied pressure to the wound. I looked up and Jae was at Trap's side, looking down at the body at their feet.

"How is he?" She was back at my side just that fast.

"G'd the fuck up," I said, sounding strong.

"It was Mayo," Jae told me, picking me and Goon's hammers up.

"My nigga stay with me." I pressed down hard, trying to stop the bleeding. "You said you was just like me." I laughed, remembering how he said that I had more lives than a cat.

"Real niggas don't die, B. We fuckin' multiply." My nigga coughed up blood and I prayed that fuckin' help was close by.

"Stay with me, my nigga!" I yelled, looking up at the cross in the church, hoping God would bless my dawg with another day.

"I've gotta get these jammies outta here," Jae said, staring down at me, tapping the heaters under her shirt. "Babi, yuh ear mi?" Her voice interrupted my thoughts to the man above, even though I heard exactly what she had said.

"Yea, ma. Do that and take Trap with you." I knew my nigga was on the run and I wanted him to get ghost before the pigs showed up.

"I'll be back to get you," Jae announced as I kept pressure on the wound.

"Bet."

I watched as she made a dash to the exit of the church where Trap was, and within seconds they had disappeared.

"Come on, my nigga." My voice cracked as I looked down at Lil' Goon. Blood leaked from his mouth. "You can't go out like this, B." I heard the sirens so clearly that I glanced back up at the cross, telling the man above *thank you* with a head nod.

JAE

"How the nigga, sis?" Trap asked me as I pulled out the parking lot in a hurry. I could hear the sirens, so I pressed the gas pedal all the way to the floor.

"G'd the fuck up, according to Rocket." I eased up off the gas as I approached the red light, then lifted my body up a little so I could remove the gats from my waist.

Fire trucks, ambulances, and NYPD police cars ran the red light in front of me as I handed all but one hammer over to Trap.

"I pray to God that the little nigga makes it," I said out loud.

"Fo sho. But real niggas live, even when they die, sis."

The light changed and I pulled off. I knew exactly what he meant by that. Yea, Tray was long gone, but he'd forever live within us.

"Damn right, they do!" I glanced over at him in time to see a huge smile covering his face. Tray was gone, but he'd never be forgotten.

***

We made it to the crib within minutes before my cell phone rang.

"Hello," I answered as I pulled into the driveway without looking to see who the caller was.

"Jae!"

"MiMi?" My heart thumped from the panic that I heard in her voice.

"Come get me," she cried.

"Where are you?" I handed Trap the extra burner, hoping that I wouldn't regret giving it to him as he exited the car on his phone.

"At home." She mumbled, "Mommie—" and then I heard the stupid bitch.

"Who the fuck you talkin' to?" Ashanti screamed, just before the line went dead.

"Trap, I gotta go get MiMi!" I threw the car in reverse before he had a chance to answer me or close the door.

Rocket warned the dumb bitch not to mistreat his seed, but from the sound of MiMi's voice, it seemed like her dumb ass mother didn't listen.

I hit Rocket's line but got his voicemail.

"Babi, I'ma come get you right after I pick MiMi up." I ended the call. I didn't want to add more fire to what he had going on with his hood nigga. I could handle this for him; that's what he had me for. I was his bloodclath rida, and this bitch was gonna respect it or check it, today.

***

I slammed the car door once I was out the parked car. The bitch left the front door wide open, so I just walked in, pinning my hair up in a ponytail.

"MiMi," I called out.

I slammed the car door once I was out the parked car. The bitch left the front door wide open, so I just walked in, pinning my hair up in a ponytail. "MiMi," Ii called again, but she didn't answer. I closed the front door and turned around, only to be staring at Ashanti with a gun in her hand.

"Yea, bitch!" She yelled, feeling powerful with the gun aimed at me. Her hands were shaking and I knew the bitch was scared.

"Where MiMi?" I asked her, but her eyes didn't leave my stomach. "Huh?" I snapped towards her.

"Stop. Fuckin'. Moving!" She steadied the gun at my head. "You pregnant?"

I stopped walking, frustrated that I gave Trap my piece. *Fuck!* I screamed inside. I'd never been without protection.

"Bitch, you're pregnant." She answered the question herself. "Rocket just had to have you, huh?" She kept going.

"Yea!" I snapped my neck and cracked my knuckles. Fuck her and that pistol. I've gotten hit up before.

"MiMi!" I yelled, ready to leave 'cause the bitch wasn't about to do shit but run her fucking mouth.

"Jae?" MiMi came limping down the stairs.

Seeing this, and knowing her bitch ass mother had hurt her, I spazzed out. "Bitch, I'm about to fuck you up!"

I charged at Ashanti.

Boom!

The loud, sudden sound made me stop in my tracks.

ROCKET

I watched the paramedics load Goon into the ambulance from afar. Brad ran into the church and let me know that the people were pulling up.

"How he do?"

"Little nigga's a G. He's gonna make it," I informed him.

The police were wrapping yellow tape around the place, near Mayo's dead body.

"Man, that shit happened so fast, yo."

A nigga had to stay ready for war at all times. "It's all good. Our nigga still breathing. The enemy is dead." Then, I dialed Jae's number, keeping my eyes on the police.

"Hello?" It wasn't Jae who answered. The voice was of someone who was hysterical.

I started moving toward Brad's ride with my brows knitted. "Who's this?"

"Daddy, it's MiMi!"

"What's wrong, baby girl?"

"No!" someone screamed in the background.

"MiMi!" I barked.

"Mommie shot Jae!" she screamed.

I froze dead in my tracks. My heart stopped beating as MiMi repeated her words even stronger.

"Mommie shot Jae!"

"No! No! My baby!"

To Be Continued…
Blood Stains of a Shotta 3
Coming Soon

ACKNOWLEDMENTS

Lord, it's me again. Thank you. Thank you. Thank you. I know you control everything that goes on with me and around me. I thank you for that. No matter how hard I fall, you pick me up, you embrace me with nothing but pure LOVE. And when my road get's cloudy, you shine that light down on me to let me know that you'll never leave nor forsake me. Artist: Luciano... Song: It's Me Again Jah

Julia James, Mama, I love you with all of my heart. Thank you for taking the time out to raise me like you gave birth to me. And for the record, you did an amazing job. Thank you for teaching me the simple things, your love, guidance and loyalty will live forever in me. I am who I am because of you and I thank you for that! I LOVE YOU with all of me. Artist: Garnett Silk... Song: Mama

Tameia Davis, My twin, I love you and I miss you something bad, but I'm glad we communicate the way we do, eeryday(your word). I love all your rap songs, real talk, the things that you be spittin' breaks my heart cause it's nothing but the truth. I love ya realness. My blood is running thru you, so I know you gonna be GREAT at everything that you put your mind towards. I LOVE YOU... Artist: Boosie... Song: I'm Sorry

Leather, thank you for stopping your life to raise my kids. I owe you a lot, shit, I owe you everything cause they are my world, my all, my life. Thank you and I LOVE YOU.

Gevetta, Mane what a journey, what a bond we have. I LOVE YOU, real talk. You've got so much faith in me that it's crazy. You give me the truth all the time, I know you don't really like me writing about the streets, but the streets will always be apart of me. But I promise you, I'm going to get it together. I love you, always and forever.

Shawn Walker, Ayo, I miss you, but I want you to know that the LOVE will never change. I salute you, I admire your loyalty and your strength. You've been thru it but you still standing. G'd all the way up like the warrior that you are. I LOVE YOU, know that. And if a muthalove test yuh, yuh already know I'm there. Artist: Jeezy... Song: Like Them

Keke Culpepper aka Mizz Polo... Sissy, what it do with you? Ayo, you got 1 year left yo. You knocked them joints down like nothing. Mane, I'm hella happy for you. I can't wait to blow ya phone, inbox, mailbox and all that up. Shyt, you know they can't hold a REAL bitch forever. Thanks for riding this joint with me from the inside. I truly wish I could have took that charge for you. Loyalty is what we are made of. I LOVE YOU, sissy. We bonded by loyalty, nigga. Artist: Jeezy(I know you love Gotti, but he don't go hard as Jeezy :)... Song: Spyder

La'Tasha Wilkins- Flowsicka, shit is crazy, I never expected that shit to happen to you like it did, but I

know you all the way 1 hunnid and nothing can change you. I'ma stay screaming #freeflowsicka. Keep writing them songs, you gonna blow up. Effff it, let me drop one of ya joint right now.
"These bitches hate me cause I bubble
Counting bands up make it double
I can show you bitches how to hustle
Money coming in by the duffel
Sipping Magaritas with Reeka that bitch a geeker
Politicking on the ave with Tameka blowing that reefa
Switching lanes in the charger with Shauna dodging them haters
Me and Ms. Jamaica some chasers we got that paper
Now I'm in a celly with Melly making them jelly..."
Yo, hold ya head. We bonded by LOYALTY, sissy. I LOVE YOU. Artist: Flowsicka... Song: Bubble

Tianna aka The Blanket QUEEN. You are #TeamJamaica, hands down. Thank you for having my back the way you do, real talk. When I got here to Alderson WV, you put me up on game like we were on the street, showed me the in's and out like water, but that's what real bitches do though. I thank you for that. When I am grinding (with the 1 jobs that I have) you are there reminding me what I need to do, thanks. When them haters tried to put me out of the wack ass library about a type writer, you told me to chill... LOL... The very next day you got me my own type writer (hahahah). Girl, you are crazy! Anything I need, you are there! I pray that our bond will last forever, real talk. I LOVE YOU! I'm going to be sad when you leave in 23 days but I know you gonna keep in touch and I'm Jeezy with that. I am excited for you to be home with your family. #RealBitchFromPhilly# Artist: Jeezy... Song: Been Getting Money

Let me put this out there now. If I missed a name don't get in ya feelings, today is the 25 and the book will be out on the 31st and I'm just doing this(SMH) cause I hate writing one. Ca$h said it best, "If you miss one name, you'll have an arched enemy," sad but true. I don't really care though, join the list. It's muthalovin' 3am and I haven't been to sleep... #FREEALLOFY'ALL# Jasmine Rucker (Juicy, Mane, I LOVE YOU, your blood is my sissy, hold ya head, you at the door, NOW), Brandi. J(Chuck, day for day, damn YO), Diamond(I'm so proud of YOU), Asia(You are crazy, but I LOVE YOU), Shannon. R(I'm ya only prison kid, stay strong and I LOVE YOU), Mona and Jacklyn(I love y'all), Jasmine(Baby Jamaica, you're the best, thanks for keeping my hair appointment book loaded, I am always BOOK), Kearrah(You're so unique, inside joke), Ashanti(You're a great friend), Jasmine(Jazz, da love is real), Jackie. S(You're the same all the time), Jessica(I&I, I'm going to miss you, stay the same), ReRe(I love the style and hell no, you can't kill me over a BOOK, lmao #TeamJamaica), Nicole. J(thanks for buying my joints), Brittney. B(you buy all my books and don't even read them, thanks), Yady(thanks for the love. Naomi, hello), Rae(Haha Cleveland stand UP), Channel(you @ the door), Ms. Rosyln(your spirit is great), Ms. E(thanks for always checking on me), Ms.

Michelle(for always making me smile), Ms. Merlin(I love you, lady), Ms. Diana(you're amazing), Ms.Betty(you're funny), Ms. Perry(you love them hair styles), Keke(you're too damn funny), Octavia(crazy on the low, you hide it well, lol), Montrell. C(Trell, you are a trip), Rocky(I miss you friend, stay UP), La'Shonda. H(Hold ya head), Anja(Bunkie, I miss you and our late nights game of scrabble. I am the CHAMP), La'Tasha(Tee, stay strong), Dee(my bunkie NOW. The trap never stop jumping as you can see), Mona(my old bunkie, you're tri pola :)), Ms. Golden(thank you for showing love), Ms.Bryd-Benett(thanks). Mane, I'm getting tired. Taylor(you gonna make it, I got the same #), Kayla. B(Hold ya head, you got this), Katie(you are so humble), Kia. M(VA stand up), Cynthia. L(Lynchburg baby), AD(plumber of the year, lmao), Delarosa(I know my spelling off, lol), Jamaica(Chi-Chi, I love ya name), Leanna(It's nothing but THE LAND love from you), Megan(Relax), Morgan(We was bunkie and didn't talk for 6 months, YOU are CRAZY), Heather(we beefing right now), Wrandra(Franklin, haha, Jeezy time), Maggie(Meg, you always help me out when I'm doing my plumbing work in the unit), Amanda(my side neighbor, the fruits are that and you know I need them), Yvonne(Real FL love), Tasha(Freckles, I love how you look out for me. Eat real good), Jackie(My neighbor, them plugs are great), Terry(B3 here, baby), Delores(You are always smiling)------ Alright, my brain shutting down. If I left you out add it here ____________ and don't take it to ya heart. It's still LOVE with me...

Ms. Hayeward, Ms. K. Fogus, Ms. C. Ryder. LT. St. John--- Never change who y'all are.

To all the FEMALES on the GREATEST label ever: LDP:
Coffee, LOVE KNOWS NO BOUNDARIES (1-3), You smoked that series. I can't wait to read Torn Between Two (haha). I know that joint probably gonna have me crying and laughing. You are a BEAST, know that!
Nikki Tee, THESE NIGGAS AIN'T LOYAL, sad but true...
Jamila Mathis: ADDICTED TO THE DRAMA-Sunnin'
Jelissa Edwards, IF LOVIN YOU IS WRONG-Outstanding
Destiny Skai, BRIDE OF A HUSTLA series, I couldn't put em down, where the hell is 3 at?
Bre Hayes, PUSH IT TO THE LIMIT, you did just that!
Meesha, A DISTINGUISHED THUG STOLE MY HEART, boy, you did that!
Adrienne, WHEN A GOOD GIRL GOES BAD, haha, she gone forever... I loved it
Royal Nicole, BOSS'N UP series, had me up. GREAT!
Destiny J, I LOVE YOU TO DEATH, that joint had me tight.
Sonovia, BROOKLYN ON LOCK, damn right, BK on lock...

Misty Holt, I RIDE FOR MY HITTA, you did that...
MiMi, I'm about to get into LIPSTICK KILLAH...
Nicole, I'm loving A DRUG KING AND HIS DIAMOND
LOCK DOWN PUBLICATIONS and CA$H PRESENTS the HOTTEST!!!
Artist: Jeezy... Song: Just Win

To my personal assistant, Jessica, thank YOU! I don't know what I would really do without you. I love you and I thank you, real talk. I can't wait to touch so we can link back UP. Get ready! www.textingforyou.com is the GREATEST. Jess and her team can do anything for you from behind the wall, add them to ya corrlinks--- text4unow@gmail.com and let them help you. Real talk, they ARE that!

To my hater. I know haters respect hater and they flock up. I've got so many it's crazy. Damn! I don't have that hating virus in my blood so know that hating shyt ain't doing nothing but motivating me. Y'all came from a hating blood line so what do I expect? Haha, it's another 1! Guess what, I be hearing y'all comments, "that bitch can hustle"... Haha... Artist: Jeezy... Song: Never Settle

To my fans(Free and Caged up) thank you! The LOVE and support is real. I can't even lie. Without y'all, I don't know if I would be where I am now. Thank you. #TeamJamaica is real. I appreciate it all.

I LOVE y'all. THANK YOU. Artist: Jeezy... Song: The Life

To my favorite Rappers: Jeezy, Boosie and Yo Gotti, thanks for dropping nothing but hits. Believe me, they stay bumping through my speakers.

Rest In Peace: Tara, Ms. Pam, Ms. Robin--- I miss y'all everyday, real talk...Gone but never FORGOTTEN.

To the ones that counted me out, it's all Jeezy on this end. I am still Jeezy, will always be REAL, that shit is embedded in me. My daddy ain't wore no rubber, I was made for this shit. Artist: Jeezy... Songs: Respect and This One For You...

Feel Free to reach out to me. I will hit you back no matter what.

Face Book: Julian James

Snail Mail:

Julian Jamaica James 16692084
Po Box A-B1
Alderson, WV, 24910

#FREEALLTHEREALFEMALES

Coming Soon from Lock Down Publications/Ca$h Presents

BOW DOWN TO MY GANGSTA

By **Ca$h**

TORN BETWEEN TWO

By **Coffee**

BLOOD STAINS OF A SHOTTA **III**

By **Jamaica**

WHEN THE STREETS CLAP BACK **II**

By **Jibril Williams**

STEADY MOBBIN

By **Marcellus Allen**

BLOOD OF A BOSS **V**

By **Askari**

BRIDE OF A HUSTLA **III**

By **Destiny Skai**

WHEN A GOOD GIRL GOES BAD **II**

By **Adrienne**

LOVE & CHASIN' PAPER **II**

By **Qay Crockett**

THE HEART OF A GANGSTA **III**

By **Jerry Jackson**

LOYAL TO THE GAME **IV**

By **T.J. & Jelissa**

A DOPEBOY'S PRAYER **II**

Jamaica

By **Eddie "Wolf" Lee**

IF LOVING YOU IS WRONG… **III**

By **Jelissa**

BLOODY COMMAS **III**

SKI MASK CARTEL II

By **T.J. Edwards**

BLAST FOR ME **II**

RAISED AS A GOON V

BRED BY THE SLUMS II

By **Ghost**

A DISTINGUISHED THUG STOLE MY HEART **III**

By **Meesha**

ADDICTIED TO THE DRAMA **II**

By **Jamila Mathis**

LIPSTICK KILLAH II

By **Mimi**

THE BOSSMAN'S DAUGHTERS 4

By **Aryanna**

Available Now

RESTRAINING ORDER **I & II**

By **CA$H & Coffee**

LOVE KNOWS NO BOUNDARIES **I II & III**

By **Coffee**

RAISED AS A GOON I, II, III & IV

BRED BY THE SLUMS

By **Ghost**

LAY IT DOWN **I & II**

LAST OF A DYING BREED

BLOOD STAINS OF A SHOTTA

By **Jamaica**

LOYAL TO THE GAME

LOYAL TO THE GAME II

LOYAL TO THE GAME III

By **TJ & Jelissa**

BLOODY COMMAS I & II

SKI MASK CARTEL

By **T.J. Edwards**

IF LOVING HIM IS WRONG...I & II

By **Jelissa**

WHEN THE STREETS CLAP BACK

By **Jibril Williams**

A DISTINGUISHED THUG STOLE MY HEART I & II

By **Meesha**

PUSH IT TO THE LIMIT

By **Bre' Hayes**

BLOOD OF A BOSS **I, II, III & IV**

By **Askari**

THE STREETS BLEED MURDER **I, II & III**

THE HEART OF A GANGSTA I & II

Jamaica

By **Jerry Jackson**

CUM FOR ME

CUM FOR ME 2

CUM FOR ME 3

An **LDP Erotica Collaboration**

BRIDE OF A HUSTLA **I & II**

THE FETTI GIRLS **I, II& III**

By **Destiny Skai**

WHEN A GOOD GIRL GOES BAD

By **Adrienne**

A GANGSTER'S REVENGE **I II III & IV**

THE BOSS MAN'S DAUGHTERS

THE BOSS MAN'S DAUGHTERS II

THE BOSSMAN'S DAUGHTERS III

A SAVAGE LOVE **I & II**

BAE BELONGS TO ME

A HUSTLER'S DECEIT I, II

By **Aryanna**

A KINGPIN'S AMBITON

A KINGPIN'S AMBITION **II**

I MURDER FOR THE DOUGH

By **Ambitious**

TRUE SAVAGE

TRUE SAVAGE II

TRUE SAVAGE **III**

By **Chris Green**

A DOPEBOY'S PRAYER

By **Eddie "Wolf" Lee**

THE KING CARTEL **I, II & III**

By **Frank Gresham**

THESE NIGGAS AIN'T LOYAL **I, II & III**

By **Nikki Tee**

GANGSTA SHYT **I II &III**

By **CATO**

THE ULTIMATE BETRAYAL

By **Phoenix**

BOSS'N UP **I , II & III**

By **Royal Nicole**

I LOVE YOU TO DEATH

By Destiny J

I RIDE FOR MY HITTA

I STILL RIDE FOR MY HITTA

By **Misty Holt**

LOVE & CHASIN' PAPER

By **Qay Crockett**

TO DIE IN VAIN

By **ASAD**

BROOKLYN HUSTLAZ

By **Boogsy Morina**

BROOKLYN ON LOCK I & II

Jamaica

By **Sonovia**

GANGSTA CITY

By **Teddy Duke**

A DRUG KING AND HIS DIAMOND

A DOPEMAN'S RICHES

By Nicole Goosby

BOOKS BY LDP'S CEO, CA$H

TRUST IN NO MAN

TRUST IN NO MAN 2

TRUST IN NO MAN 3

BONDED BY BLOOD

SHORTY GOT A THUG

THUGS CRY

THUGS CRY 2

THUGS CRY 3

TRUST NO BITCH

TRUST NO BITCH 2

TRUST NO BITCH 3

TIL MY CASKET DROPS

RESTRAINING ORDER

RESTRAINING ORDER 2

IN LOVE WITH A CONVICT

Coming Soon

BONDED BY BLOOD 2

BOW DOWN TO MY GANGSTA

CPSIA information can be obtained
at www.ICGtesting.com
Printed in the USA
LVHW081126110119
603318LV00028B/212/P